STONE ARCH BOOKS
a capstone imprint

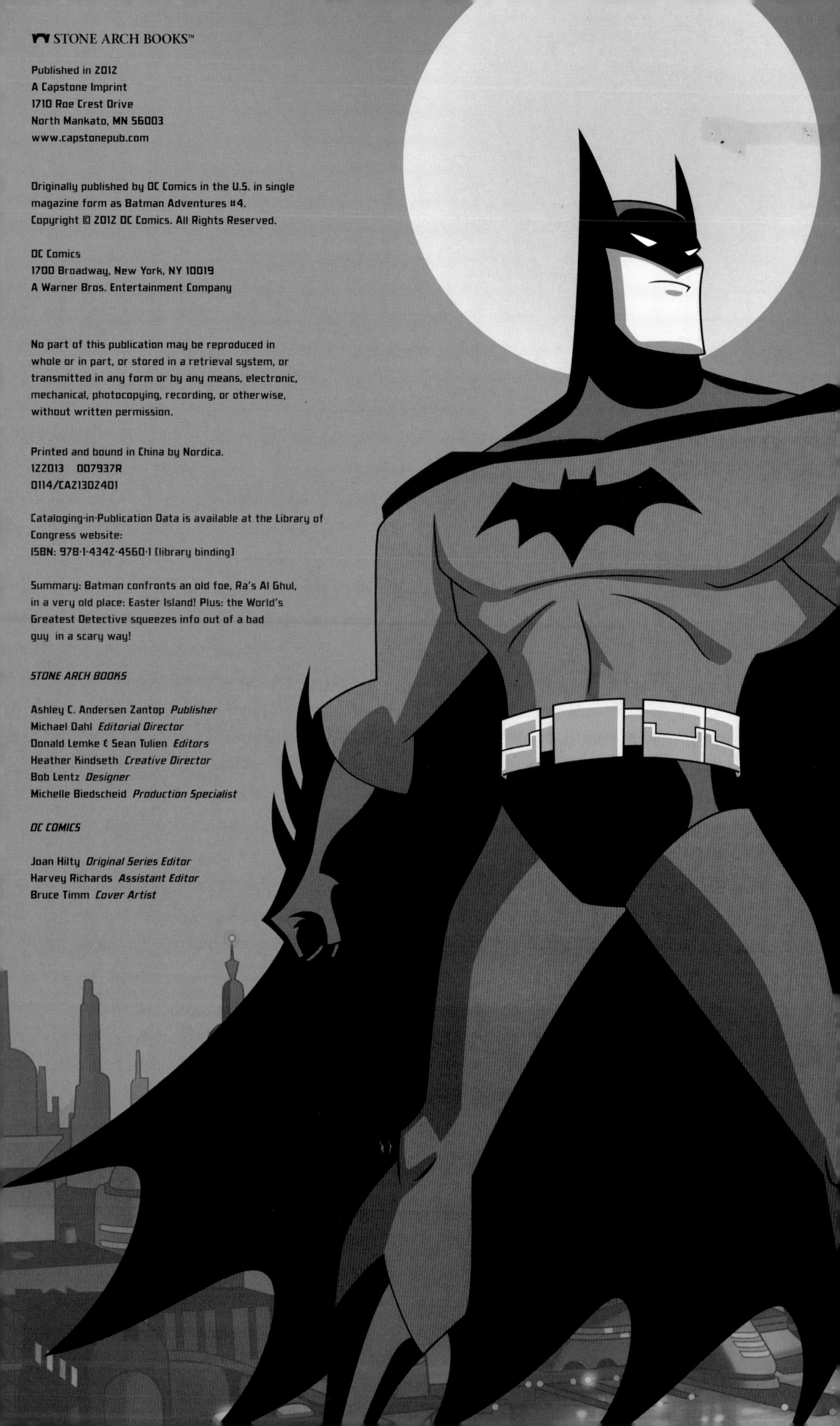

STONE ARCH BOOKS™

Published in 2012
A Capstone Imprint
1710 Roe Crest Drive
North Mankato, MN 56003
www.capstonepub.com

Originally published by DC Comics in the U.S. in single magazine form as Batman Adventures #4.

DC Comics
1700 Broadway, New York, NY 10019
A Warner Bros. Entertainment Company

Printed and bound in China by Nordica.
122013 007937R
0114/CA21302401

Cataloging-in-Publication Data is available at the Library of Congress website:
ISBN: 978-1-4342-4560-1 (library binding)

Summary: Batman confronts an old foe, Ra's Al Ghul, in a very old place: Easter Island! Plus: the World's Greatest Detective squeezes info out of a bad guy in a scary way!

STONE ARCH BOOKS

Ashley C. Andersen Zantop *Publisher*
Michael Dahl *Editorial Director*
Donald Lemke & Sean Tulien *Editors*
Heather Kindseth *Creative Director*
Bob Lentz *Designer*
Michelle Biedscheid *Production Specialist*

DC COMICS

Joan Hilty *Original Series Editor*
Harvey Richards *Assistant Editor*
Bruce Timm *Cover Artist*

BATMAN ADVENTURES

NEED TO KNOW

Ty Templeton & Dan Slott .... *writers*
Rick Burchett & Ty Templeton .... *pencillers*
Terry Beatty .... *inker*
Lee Loughridge & Zylonol Studios .... *colorists*
Phil Felix .... *letterer*

Batman created by
Bob Kane

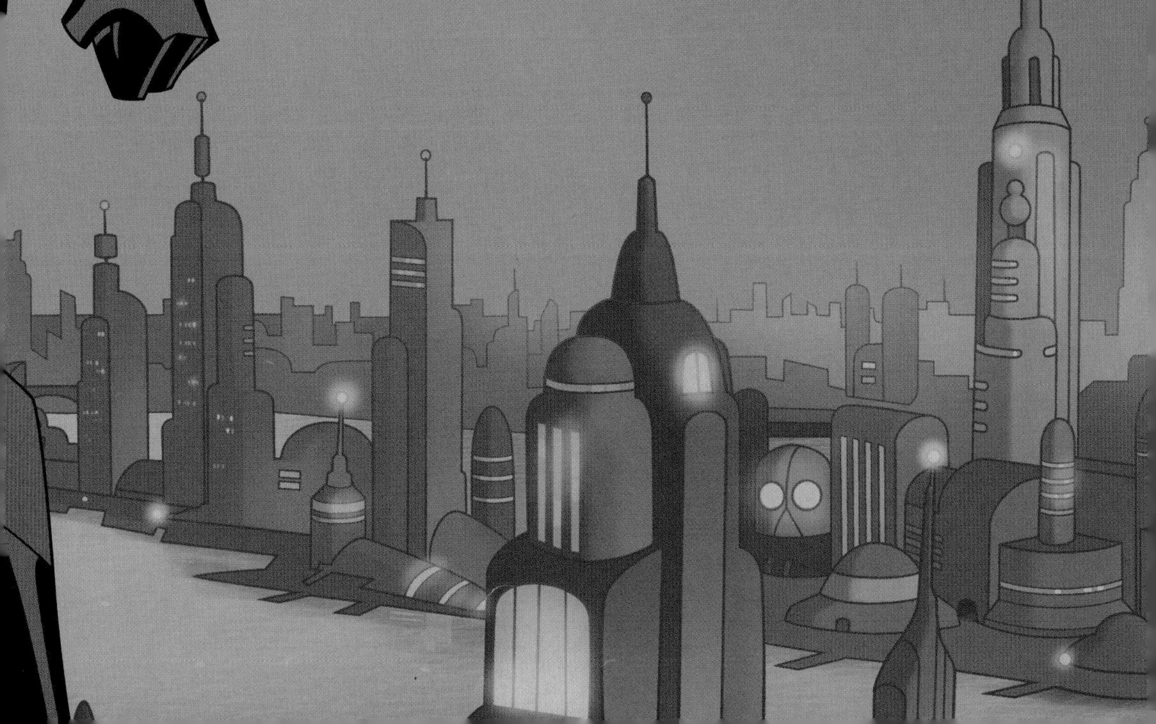

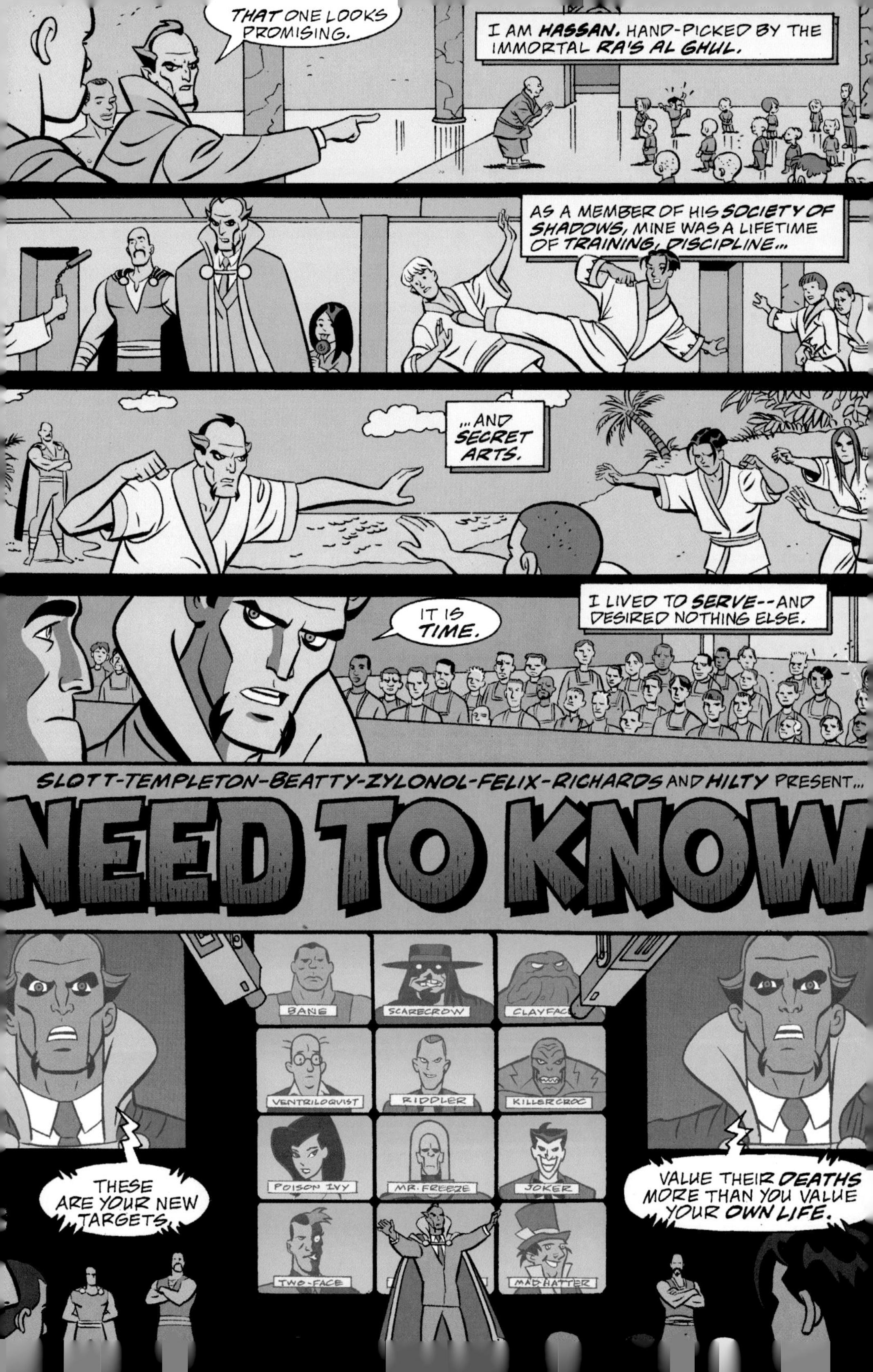
THAT ONE LOOKS PROMISING.
I AM HASSAN. HAND-PICKED BY THE IMMORTAL RA'S AL GHUL.
AS A MEMBER OF HIS SOCIETY OF SHADOWS, MINE WAS A LIFETIME OF TRAINING, DISCIPLINE...
...AND SECRET ARTS.
IT IS TIME.
I LIVED TO SERVE--AND DESIRED NOTHING ELSE.
SLOTT-TEMPLETON-BEATTY-ZYLONOL-FELIX-RICHARDS AND HILTY PRESENT...
NEED TO KNOW
BANE
SCARECROW
VENTRILOQUIST
RIDDLER
KILLER CROC
POISON IVY
MR. FREEZE
JOKER
TWO-FACE
MAD HATTER
THESE ARE YOUR NEW TARGETS.
VALUE THEIR DEATHS MORE THAN YOU VALUE YOUR OWN LIFE.

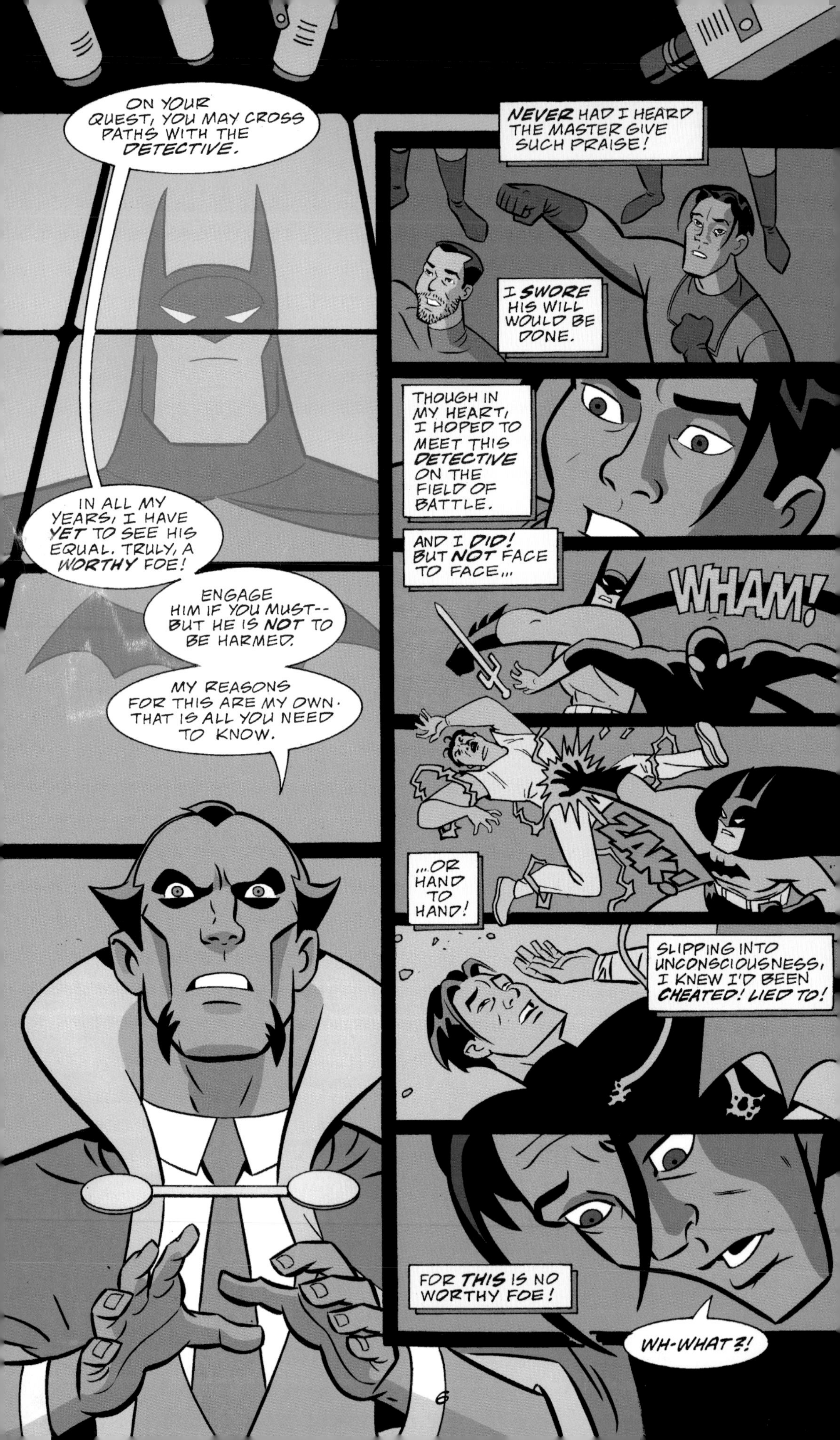

ON YOUR QUEST, YOU MAY CROSS PATHS WITH THE DETECTIVE.
IN ALL MY YEARS, I HAVE YET TO SEE HIS EQUAL. TRULY, A WORTHY FOE!
ENGAGE HIM IF YOU MUST--BUT HE IS NOT TO BE HARMED.
MY REASONS FOR THIS ARE MY OWN. THAT IS ALL YOU NEED TO KNOW.
NEVER HAD I HEARD THE MASTER GIVE SUCH PRAISE!
I SWORE HIS WILL WOULD BE DONE.
THOUGH IN MY HEART, I HOPED TO MEET THIS DETECTIVE ON THE FIELD OF BATTLE.
AND I DID! BUT NOT FACE TO FACE...
WHAM!
ZAK!
...OR HAND TO HAND!
SLIPPING INTO UNCONSCIOUSNESS, I KNEW I'D BEEN CHEATED! LIED TO!
FOR THIS IS NO WORTHY FOE!
WH-WHAT?!

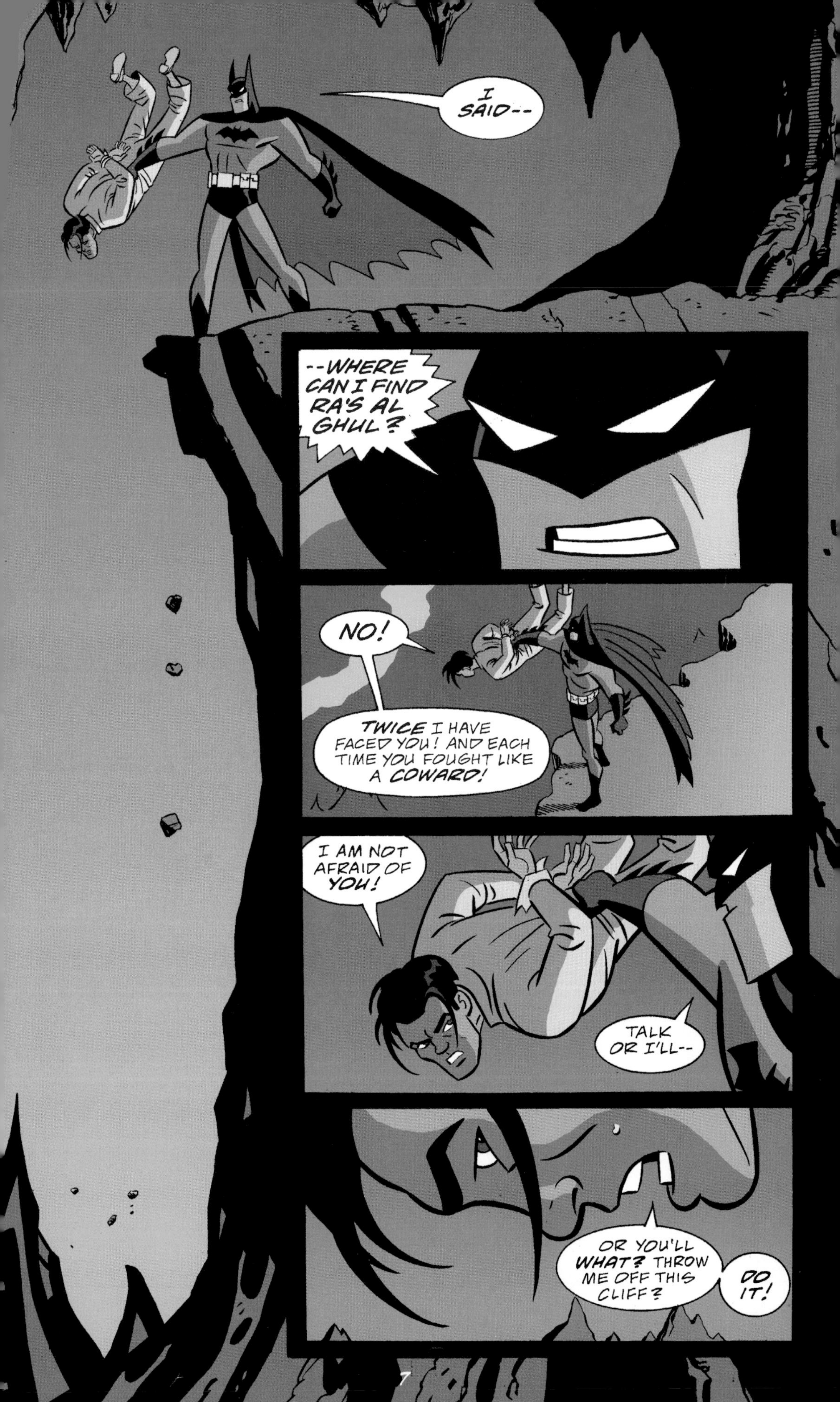
I SAID--
--WHERE CAN I FIND RA'S AL GHUL?
NO!
TWICE I HAVE FACED YOU! AND EACH TIME YOU FOUGHT LIKE A COWARD!
I AM NOT AFRAID OF YOU!
TALK OR I'LL--
OR YOU'LL WHAT? THROW ME OFF THIS CLIFF?
DO IT!

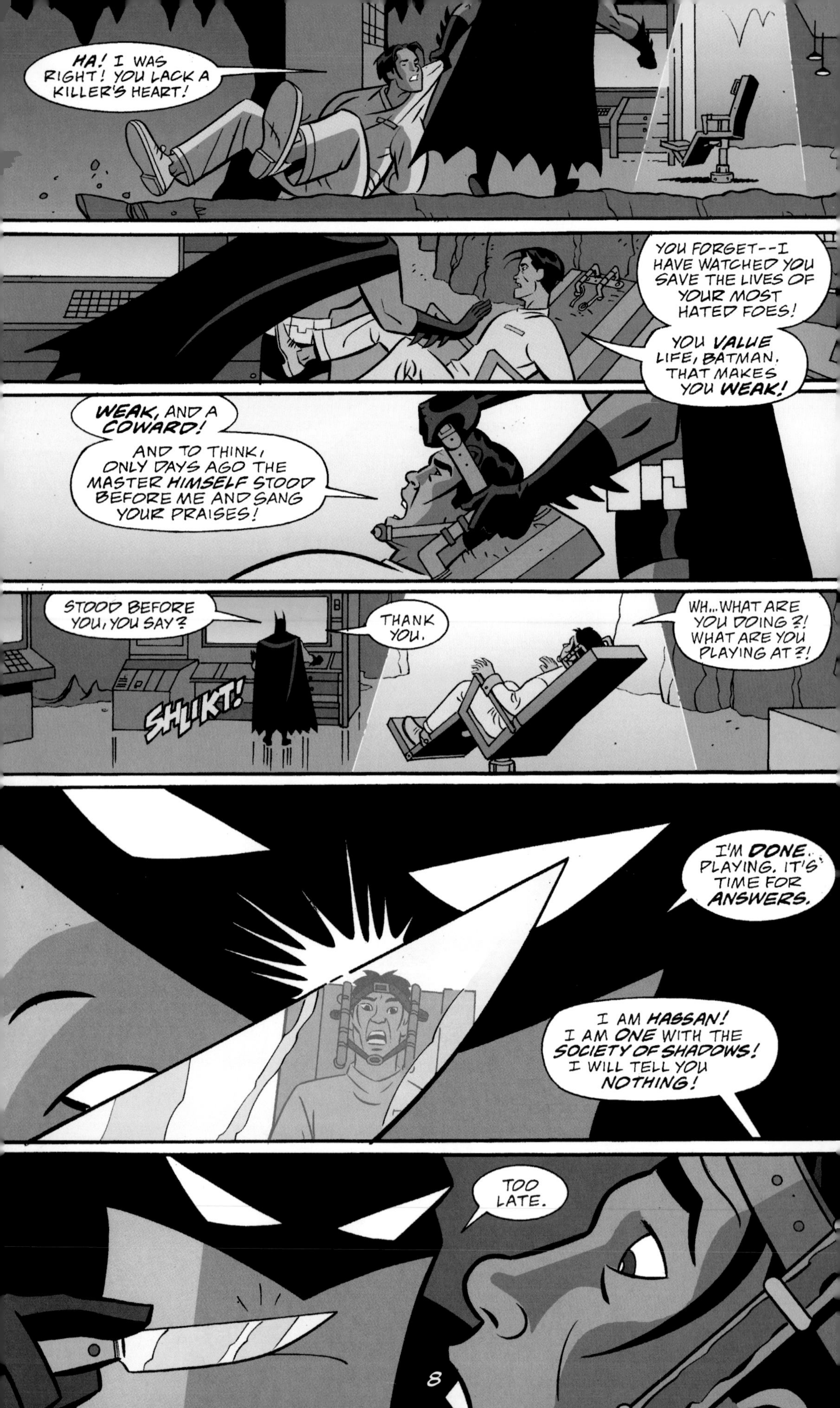
HA! I WAS RIGHT! YOU LACK A KILLER'S HEART!
YOU FORGET--I HAVE WATCHED YOU SAVE THE LIVES OF YOUR MOST HATED FOES!
YOU VALUE LIFE, BATMAN. THAT MAKES YOU WEAK!
WEAK, AND A COWARD!
AND TO THINK, ONLY DAYS AGO THE MASTER HIMSELF STOOD BEFORE ME AND SANG YOUR PRAISES!
STOOD BEFORE YOU, YOU SAY?
THANK YOU.
SHLIKT!
WH...WHAT ARE YOU DOING?! WHAT ARE YOU PLAYING AT?!
I'M DONE PLAYING. IT'S TIME FOR ANSWERS.
I AM HASSAN! I AM ONE WITH THE SOCIETY OF SHADOWS! I WILL TELL YOU NOTHING!
TOO LATE.

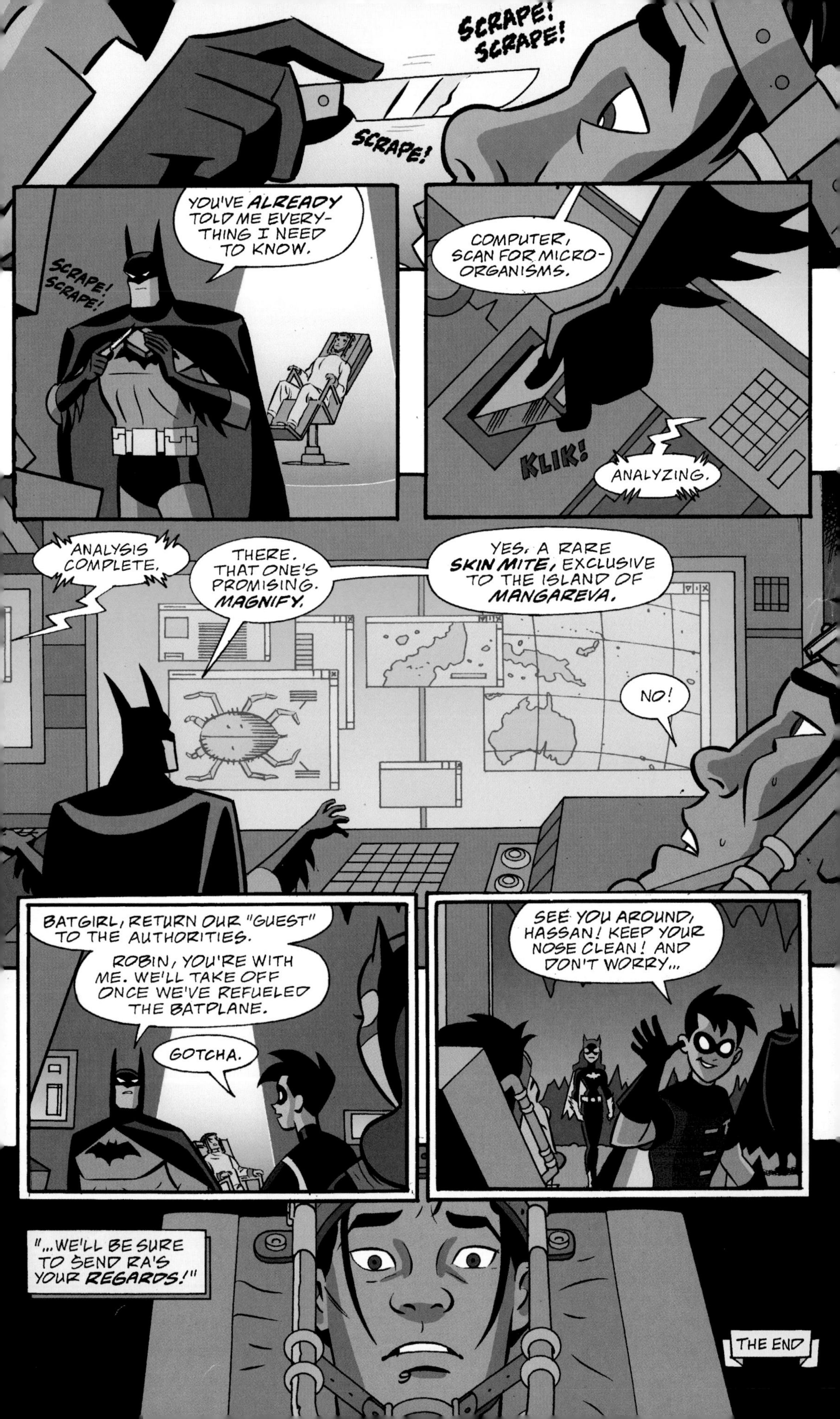
SCRAPE! SCRAPE!
SCRAPE!
SCRAPE! SCRAPE!
YOU'VE ALREADY TOLD ME EVERYTHING I NEED TO KNOW.
COMPUTER, SCAN FOR MICRO-ORGANISMS.
KLIK!
ANALYZING.
ANALYSIS COMPLETE.
THERE. THAT ONE'S PROMISING. MAGNIFY.
YES. A RARE SKIN MITE, EXCLUSIVE TO THE ISLAND OF MANGAREVA.
NO!
BATGIRL, RETURN OUR "GUEST" TO THE AUTHORITIES.
ROBIN, YOU'RE WITH ME. WE'LL TAKE OFF ONCE WE'VE REFUELED THE BATPLANE.
GOTCHA.
SEE YOU AROUND, HASSAN! KEEP YOUR NOSE CLEAN! AND DON'T WORRY...
"...WE'LL BE SURE TO SEND RA'S YOUR REGARDS!"
THE END

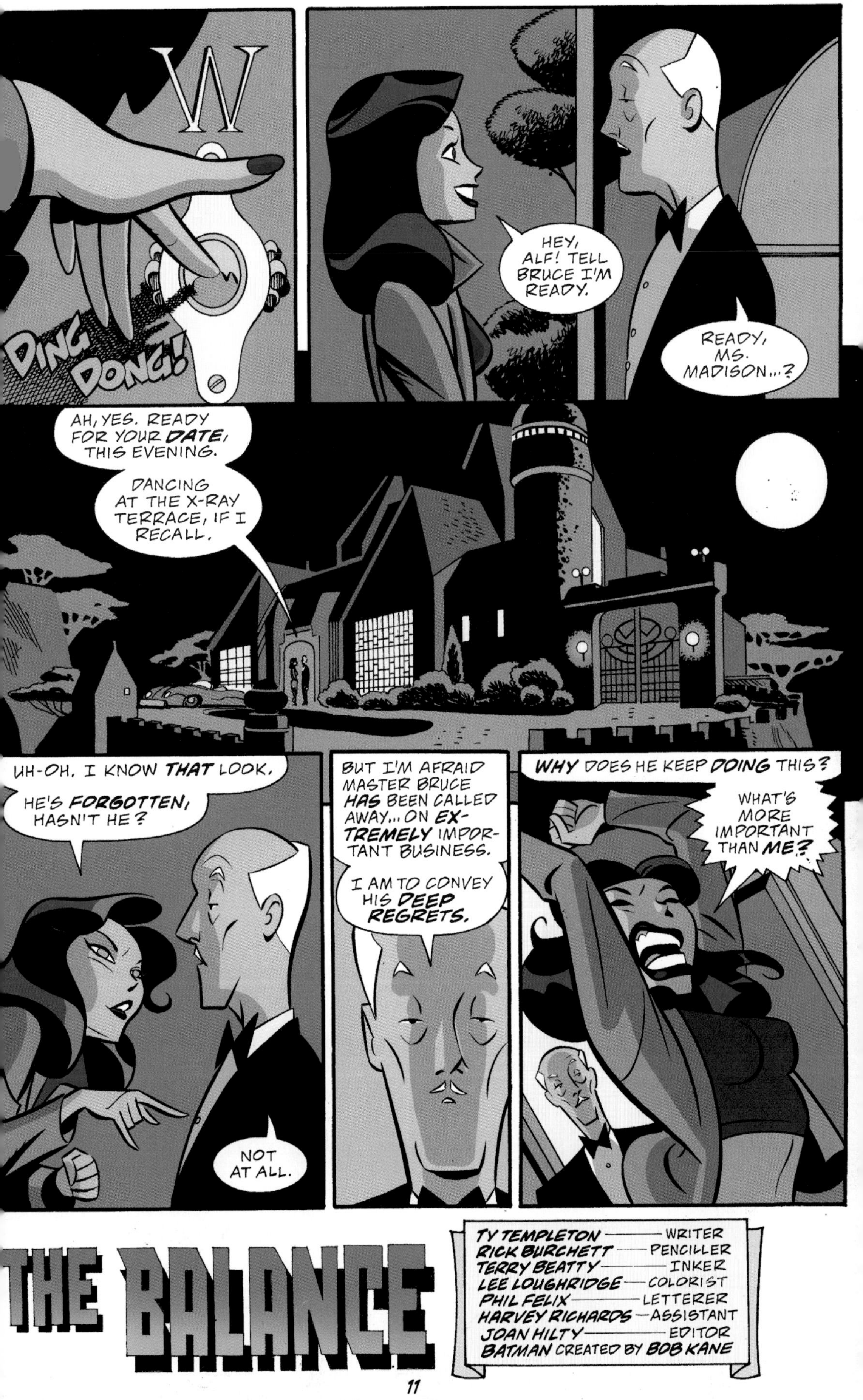
W
DING DONG!
HEY, ALF! TELL BRUCE I'M READY.
READY, MS. MADISON...?
AH, YES. READY FOR YOUR DATE, THIS EVENING.
DANCING AT THE X-RAY TERRACE, IF I RECALL.
UH-OH. I KNOW THAT LOOK.
HE'S FORGOTTEN, HASN'T HE?
NOT AT ALL.
BUT I'M AFRAID MASTER BRUCE HAS BEEN CALLED AWAY... ON EXTREMELY IMPORTANT BUSINESS.
I AM TO CONVEY HIS DEEP REGRETS.
WHY DOES HE KEEP DOING THIS?
WHAT'S MORE IMPORTANT THAN ME?

THE BALANCE

TY TEMPLETON — WRITER
RICK BURCHETT — PENCILLER
TERRY BEATTY — INKER
LEE LOUGHRIDGE — COLORIST
PHIL FELIX — LETTERER
HARVEY RICHARDS — ASSISTANT
JOAN HILTY — EDITOR
BATMAN CREATED BY BOB KANE

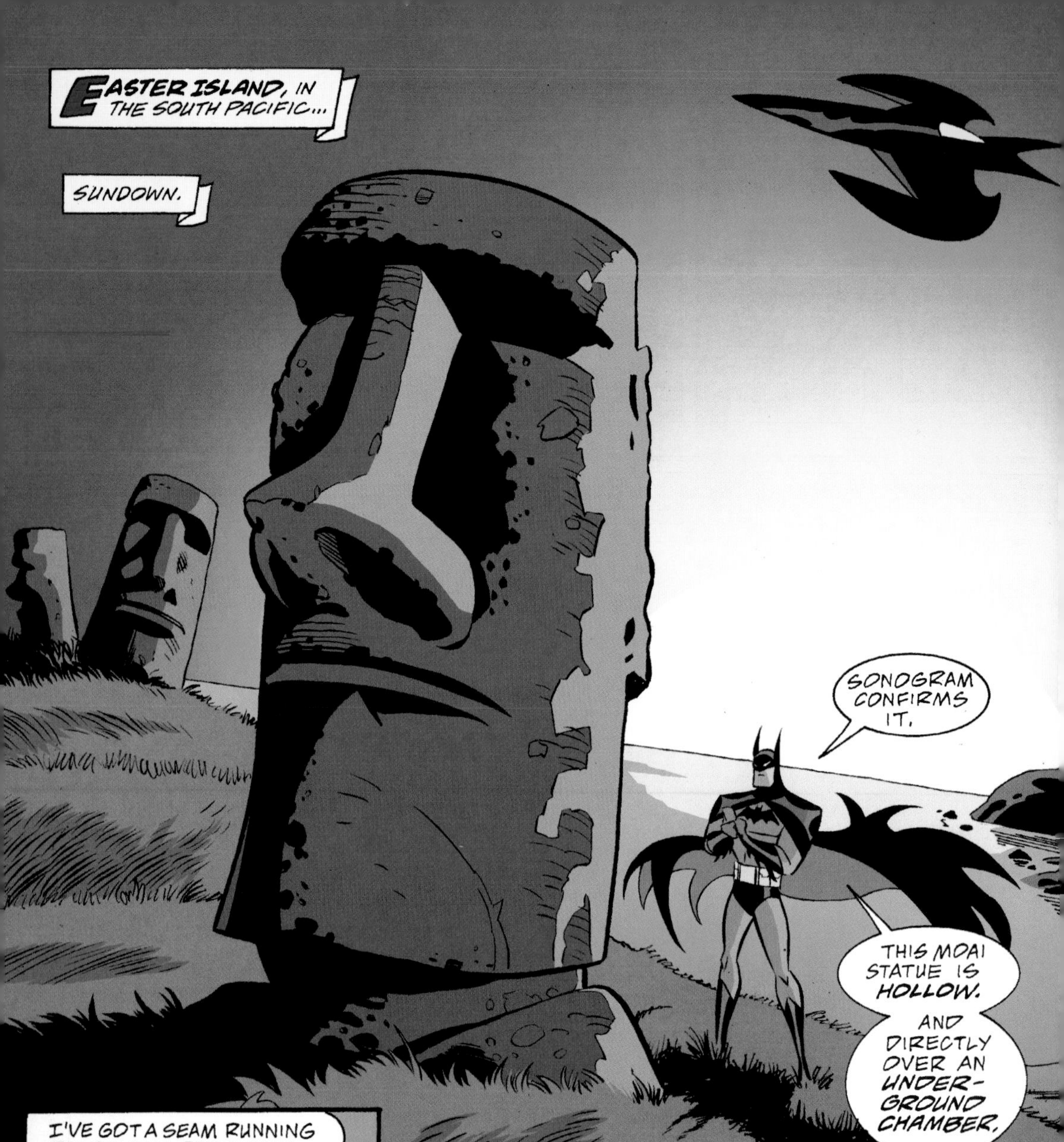
EASTER ISLAND, IN THE SOUTH PACIFIC...
SUNDOWN.
SONOGRAM CONFIRMS IT.
THIS MOAI STATUE IS HOLLOW.
AND DIRECTLY OVER AN UNDER-GROUND CHAMBER.

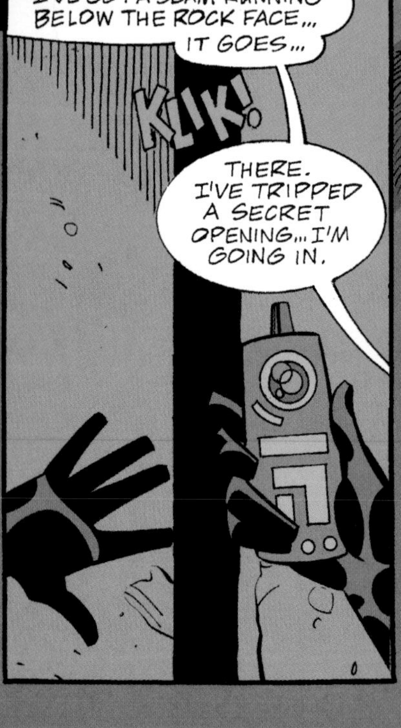
I'VE GOT A SEAM RUNNING BELOW THE ROCK FACE... IT GOES...
KLIK!
THERE. I'VE TRIPPED A SECRET OPENING... I'M GOING IN.

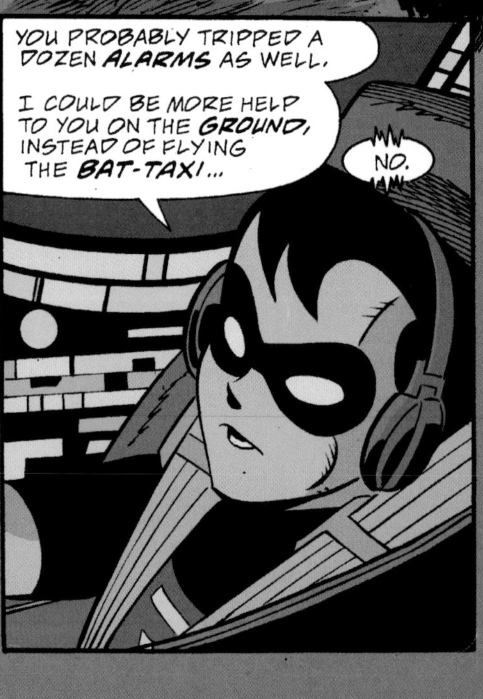
YOU PROBABLY TRIPPED A DOZEN ALARMS AS WELL.
I COULD BE MORE HELP TO YOU ON THE GROUND, INSTEAD OF FLYING THE BAT-TAXI...
NO.

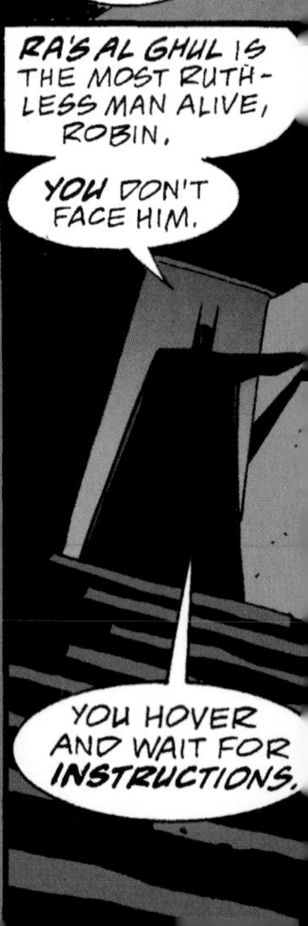
RA'S AL GHUL IS THE MOST RUTH-LESS MAN ALIVE, ROBIN.
YOU DON'T FACE HIM.
YOU HOVER AND WAIT FOR INSTRUCTIONS.

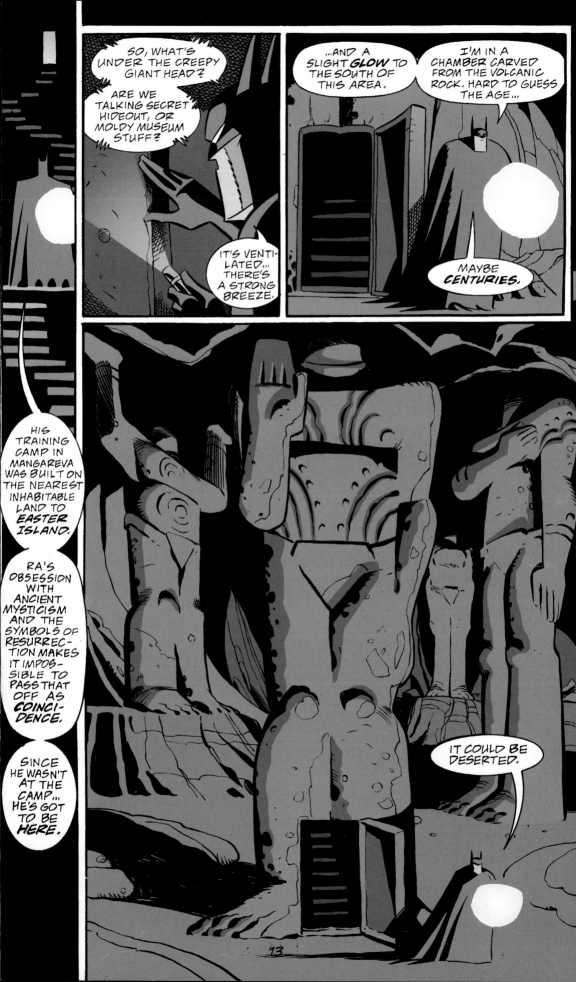

SO, WHAT'S UNDER THE CREEPY GIANT HEAD?

ARE WE TALKING SECRET HIDEOUT, OR MOLDY MUSEUM STUFF?

IT'S VENTILATED... THERE'S A STRONG BREEZE.

...AND A SLIGHT *GLOW* TO THE SOUTH OF THIS AREA,

I'M IN A CHAMBER CARVED FROM THE VOLCANIC ROCK. HARD TO GUESS THE AGE...

MAYBE *CENTURIES.*

HIS TRAINING CAMP IN MANGAREVA WAS BUILT ON THE NEAREST INHABITABLE LAND TO *EASTER ISLAND.*

RA'S OBSESSION WITH ANCIENT MYSTICISM AND THE SYMBOLS OF RESURRECTION MAKES IT IMPOSSIBLE TO PASS THAT OFF AS *COINCIDENCE.*

SINCE HE WASN'T AT THE CAMP... HE'S GOT TO BE *HERE.*

IT COULD BE DESERTED.

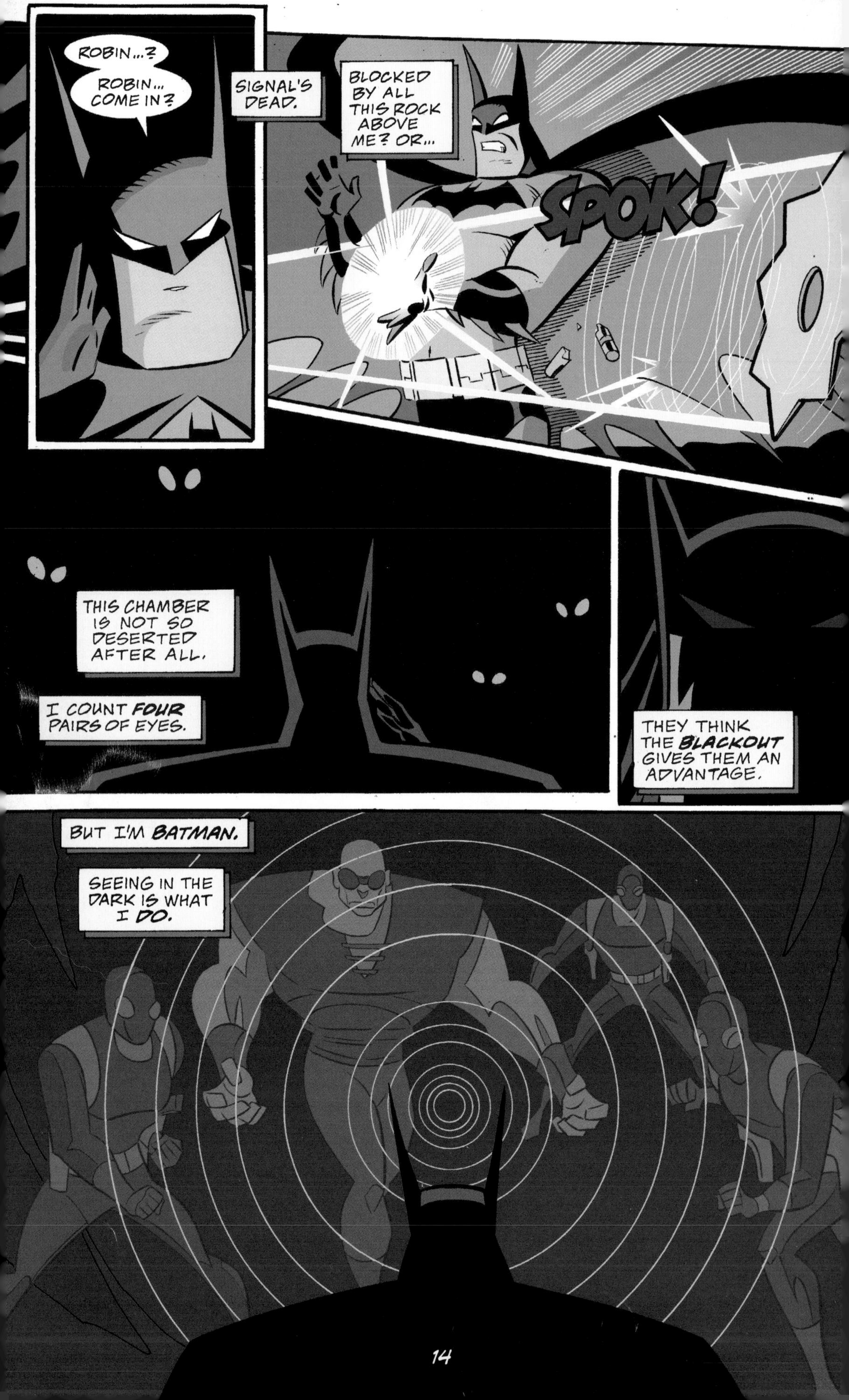
ROBIN...?
ROBIN... COME IN?
SIGNAL'S DEAD.
BLOCKED BY ALL THIS ROCK ABOVE ME? OR...
SPOK!
THIS CHAMBER IS NOT SO DESERTED AFTER ALL.
I COUNT FOUR PAIRS OF EYES.
THEY THINK THE BLACKOUT GIVES THEM AN ADVANTAGE.
BUT I'M BATMAN.
SEEING IN THE DARK IS WHAT I DO.

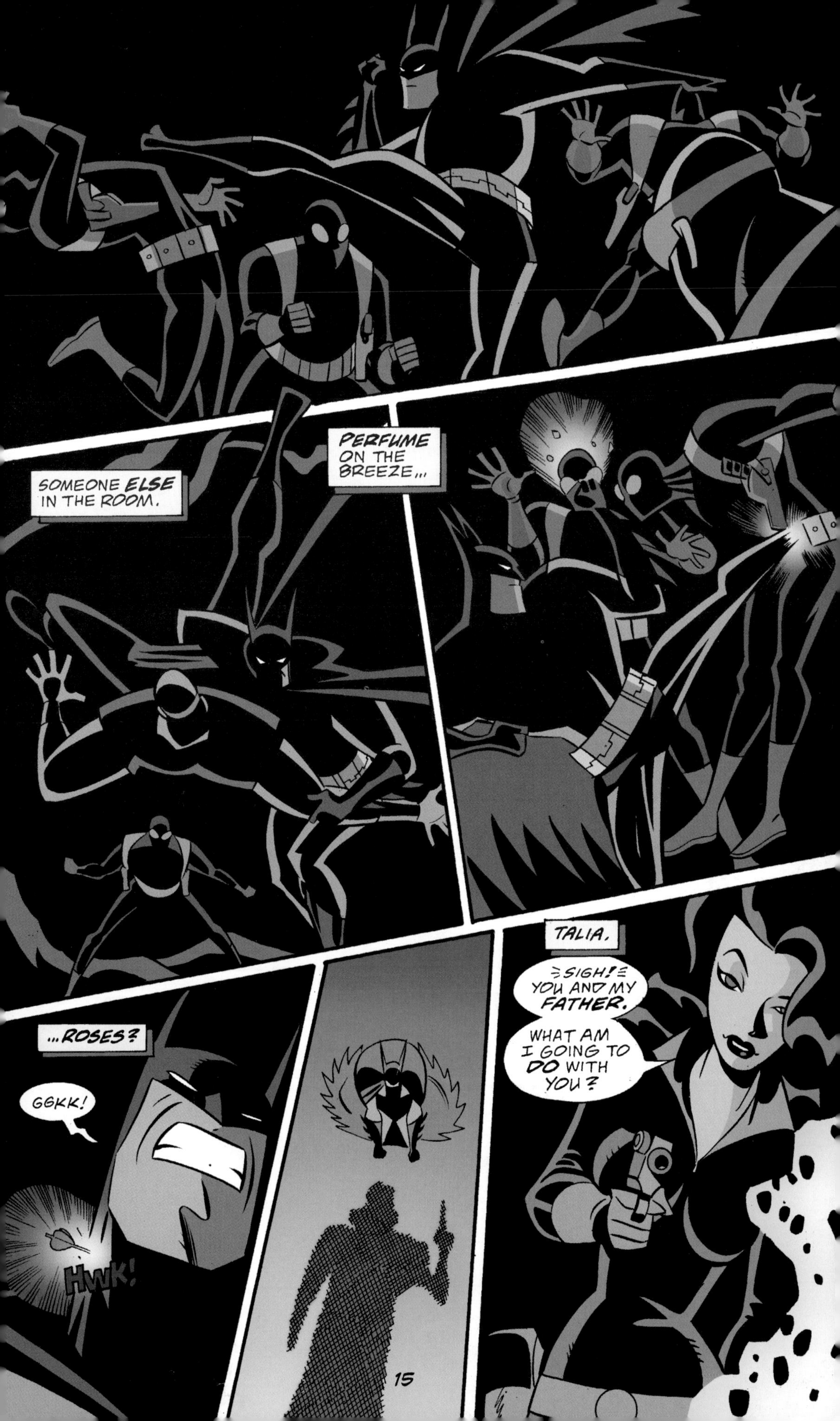

SOMEONE ELSE IN THE ROOM.
PERFUME ON THE BREEZE...
...ROSES?
GGKK!
HWK!
TALIA.
SIGH! YOU AND MY FATHER.
WHAT AM I GOING TO DO WITH YOU?

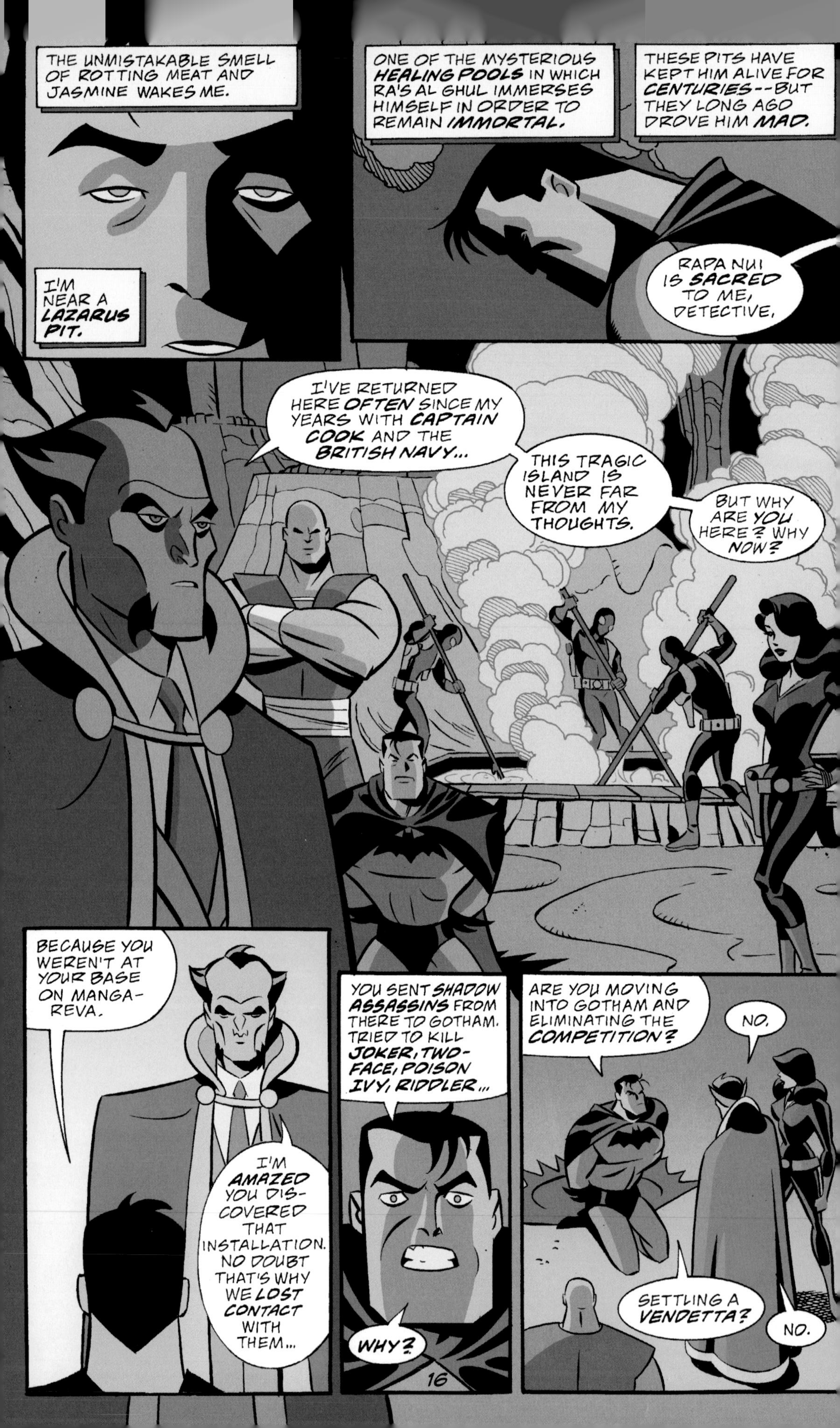
THE UNMISTAKABLE SMELL OF ROTTING MEAT AND JASMINE WAKES ME.
I'M NEAR A LAZARUS PIT.
ONE OF THE MYSTERIOUS HEALING POOLS IN WHICH RA'S AL GHUL IMMERSES HIMSELF IN ORDER TO REMAIN IMMORTAL.
THESE PITS HAVE KEPT HIM ALIVE FOR CENTURIES--BUT THEY LONG AGO DROVE HIM MAD.
RAPA NUI IS SACRED TO ME, DETECTIVE.
I'VE RETURNED HERE OFTEN SINCE MY YEARS WITH CAPTAIN COOK AND THE BRITISH NAVY...
THIS TRAGIC ISLAND IS NEVER FAR FROM MY THOUGHTS.
BUT WHY ARE YOU HERE? WHY NOW?
BECAUSE YOU WEREN'T AT YOUR BASE ON MANGA-REVA.
I'M AMAZED YOU DIS-COVERED THAT INSTALLATION. NO DOUBT THAT'S WHY WE LOST CONTACT WITH THEM...
YOU SENT SHADOW ASSASSINS FROM THERE TO GOTHAM. TRIED TO KILL JOKER, TWO-FACE, POISON IVY, RIDDLER...
WHY?
ARE YOU MOVING INTO GOTHAM AND ELIMINATING THE COMPETITION?
NO.
SETTLING A VENDETTA?
NO.

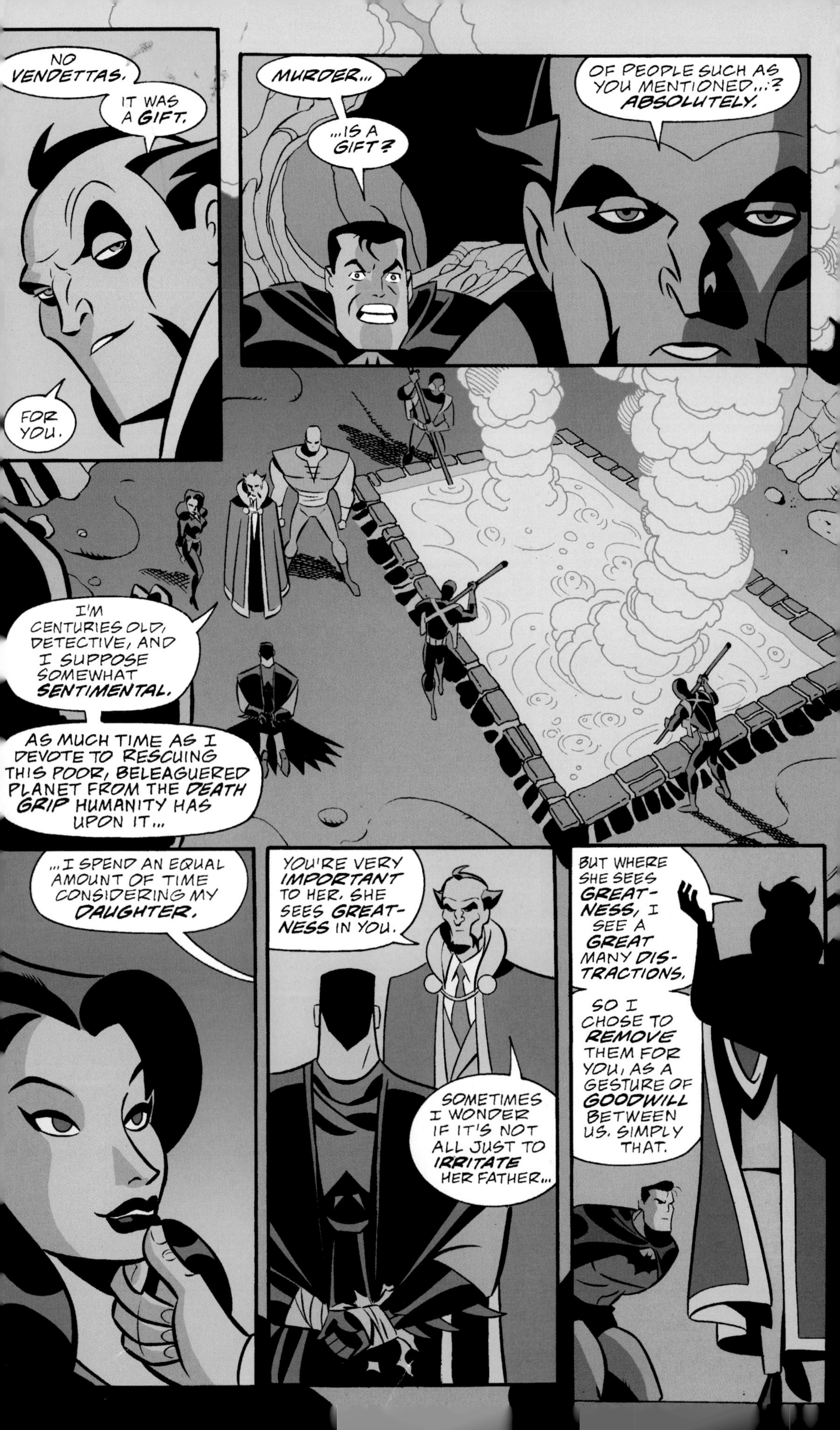
NO VENDETTAS.
IT WAS A GIFT.
FOR YOU.
MURDER...
...IS A GIFT?
OF PEOPLE SUCH AS YOU MENTIONED...? ABSOLUTELY.
I'M CENTURIES OLD, DETECTIVE, AND I SUPPOSE SOMEWHAT SENTIMENTAL.
AS MUCH TIME AS I DEVOTE TO RESCUING THIS POOR, BELEAGUERED PLANET FROM THE DEATH GRIP HUMANITY HAS UPON IT...
...I SPEND AN EQUAL AMOUNT OF TIME CONSIDERING MY DAUGHTER.
YOU'RE VERY IMPORTANT TO HER. SHE SEES GREATNESS IN YOU.
SOMETIMES I WONDER IF IT'S NOT ALL JUST TO IRRITATE HER FATHER...
BUT WHERE SHE SEES GREATNESS, I SEE A GREAT MANY DISTRACTIONS.
SO I CHOSE TO REMOVE THEM FOR YOU, AS A GESTURE OF GOODWILL BETWEEN US. SIMPLY THAT.

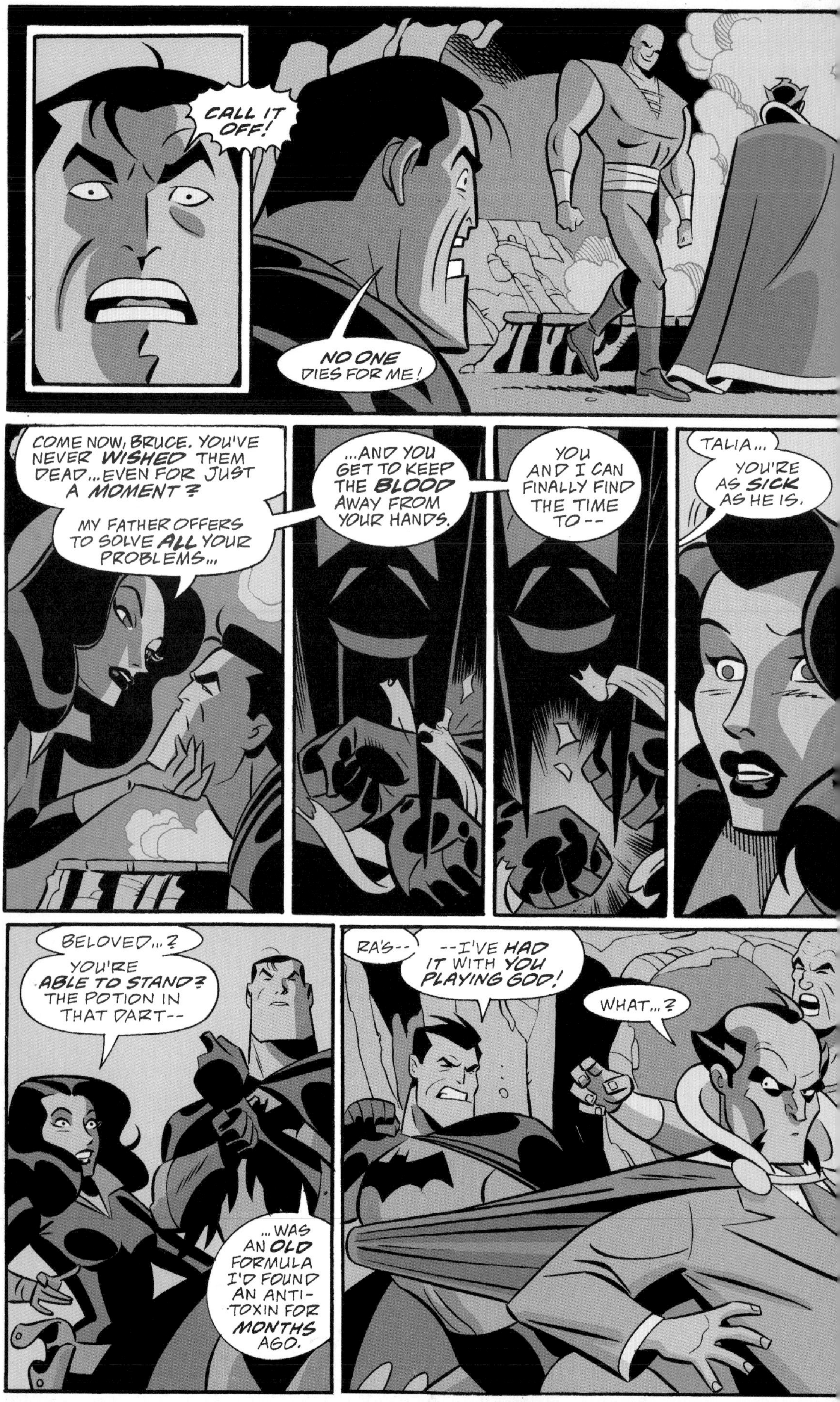
CALL IT OFF!
NO ONE DIES FOR ME!
COME NOW, BRUCE. YOU'VE NEVER WISHED THEM DEAD...EVEN FOR JUST A MOMENT?
MY FATHER OFFERS TO SOLVE ALL YOUR PROBLEMS...
...AND YOU GET TO KEEP THE BLOOD AWAY FROM YOUR HANDS.
YOU AND I CAN FINALLY FIND THE TIME TO--
TALIA...
YOU'RE AS SICK AS HE IS.
BELOVED...?
YOU'RE ABLE TO STAND? THE POTION IN THAT DART--
...WAS AN OLD FORMULA I'D FOUND AN ANTI-TOXIN FOR MONTHS AGO.
RA'S--
--I'VE HAD IT WITH YOU PLAYING GOD!
WHAT...?

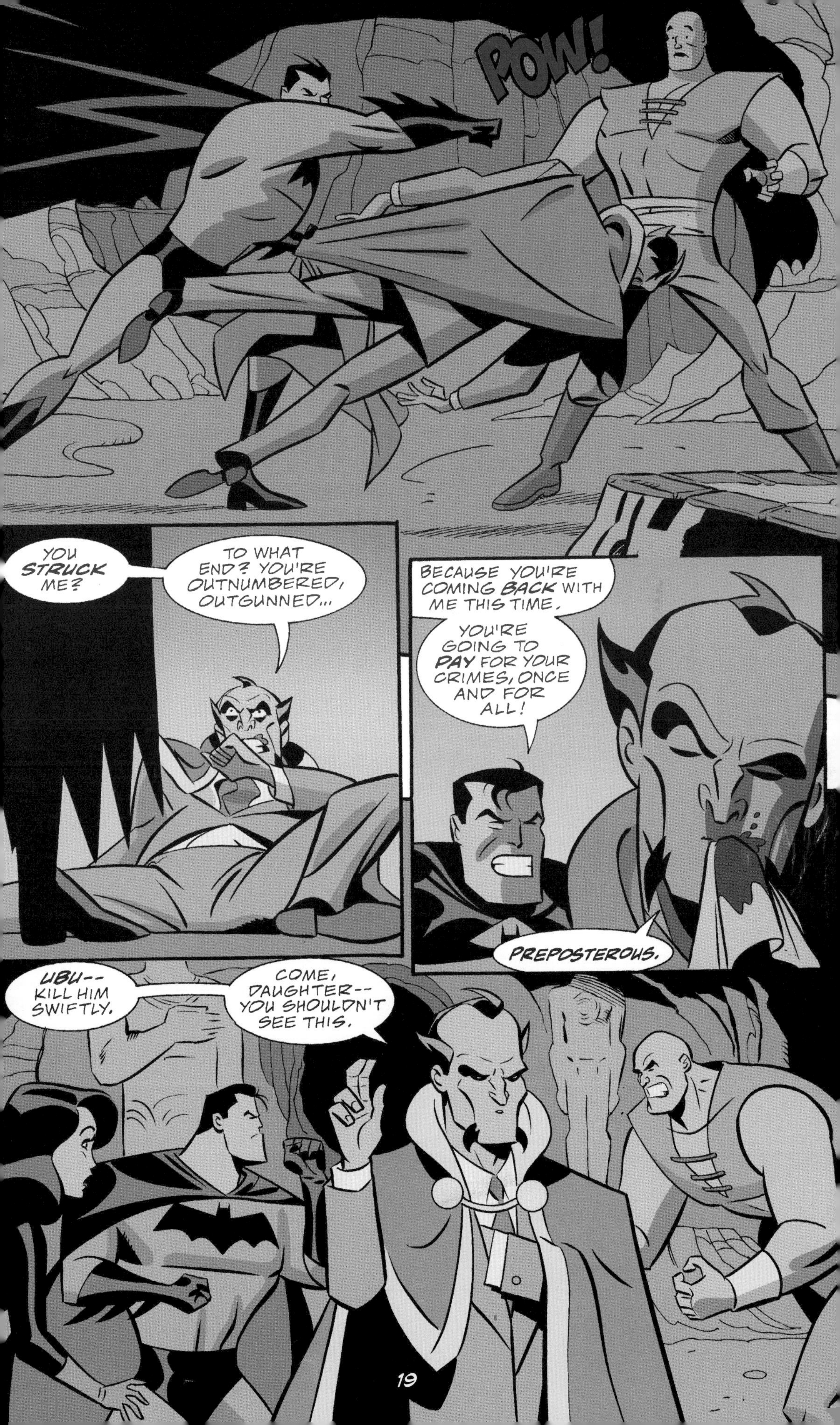
POW!
YOU STRUCK ME?
TO WHAT END? YOU'RE OUTNUMBERED, OUTGUNNED...
BECAUSE YOU'RE COMING BACK WITH ME THIS TIME.
YOU'RE GOING TO PAY FOR YOUR CRIMES, ONCE AND FOR ALL!
PREPOSTEROUS.
UBU-- KILL HIM SWIFTLY.
COME, DAUGHTER-- YOU SHOULDN'T SEE THIS.

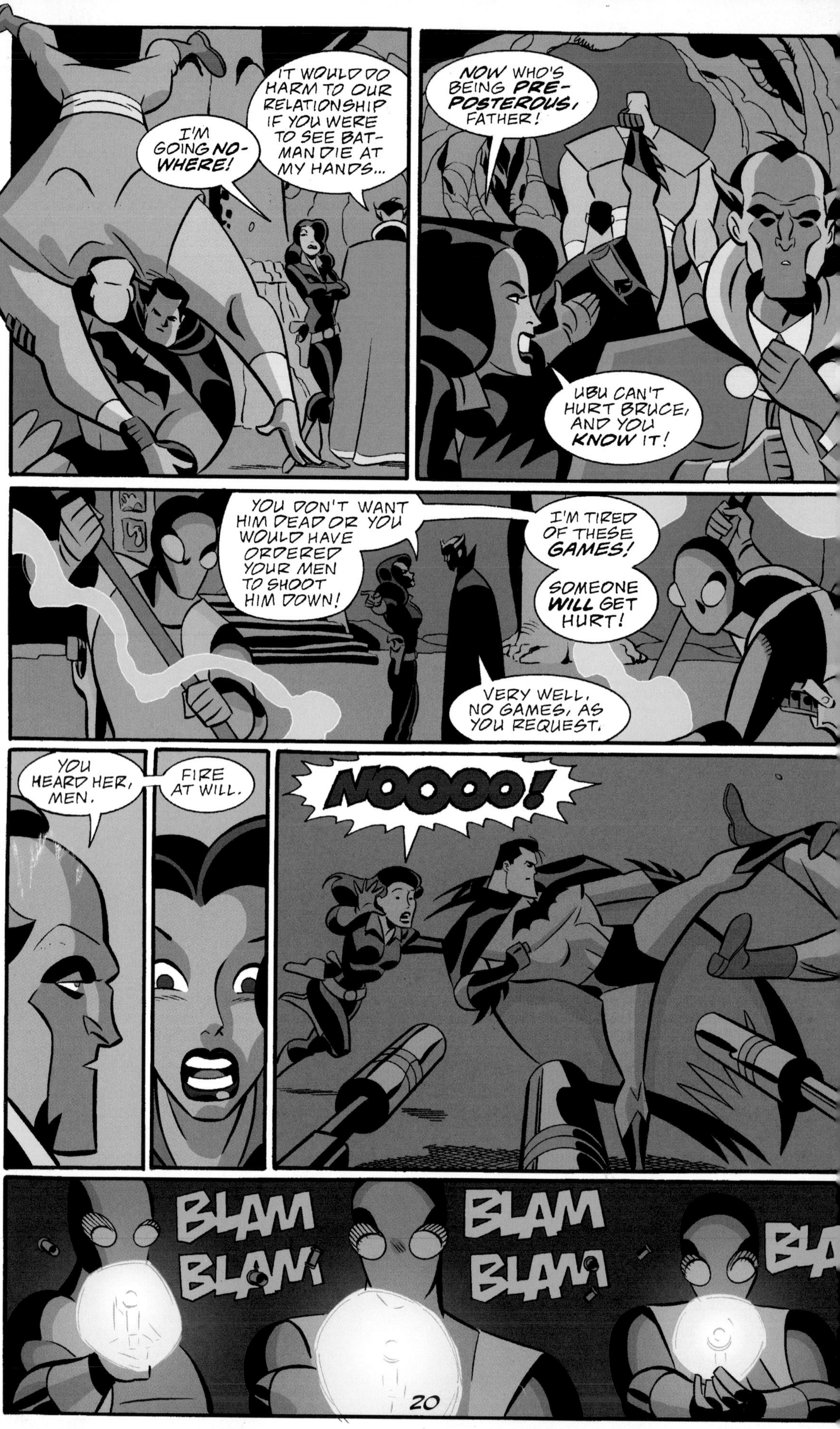

I'M GOING NOWHERE!
IT WOULD DO HARM TO OUR RELATIONSHIP IF YOU WERE TO SEE BATMAN DIE AT MY HANDS...
NOW WHO'S BEING PREPOSTEROUS, FATHER!
UBU CAN'T HURT BRUCE, AND YOU KNOW IT!
YOU DON'T WANT HIM DEAD OR YOU WOULD HAVE ORDERED YOUR MEN TO SHOOT HIM DOWN!
I'M TIRED OF THESE GAMES!
SOMEONE WILL GET HURT!
VERY WELL, NO GAMES, AS YOU REQUEST.
YOU HEARD HER, MEN.
FIRE AT WILL.
NOOOO!
BLAM
BLAM
BLAM
BLAM

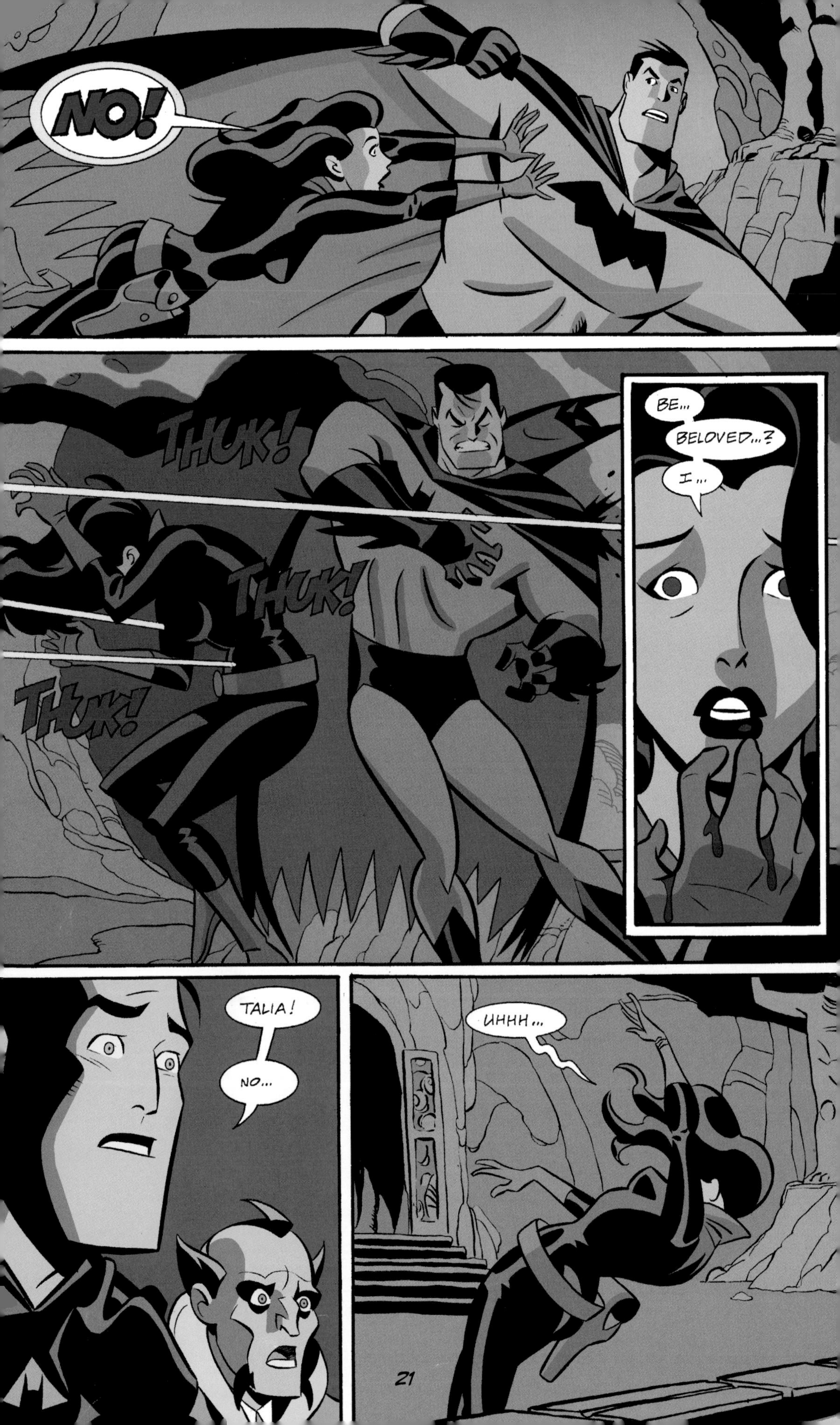
NO!
THUK!
THUK!
THUK!
BE...
BELOVED...?
I...
TALIA!
NO...
UHHH...

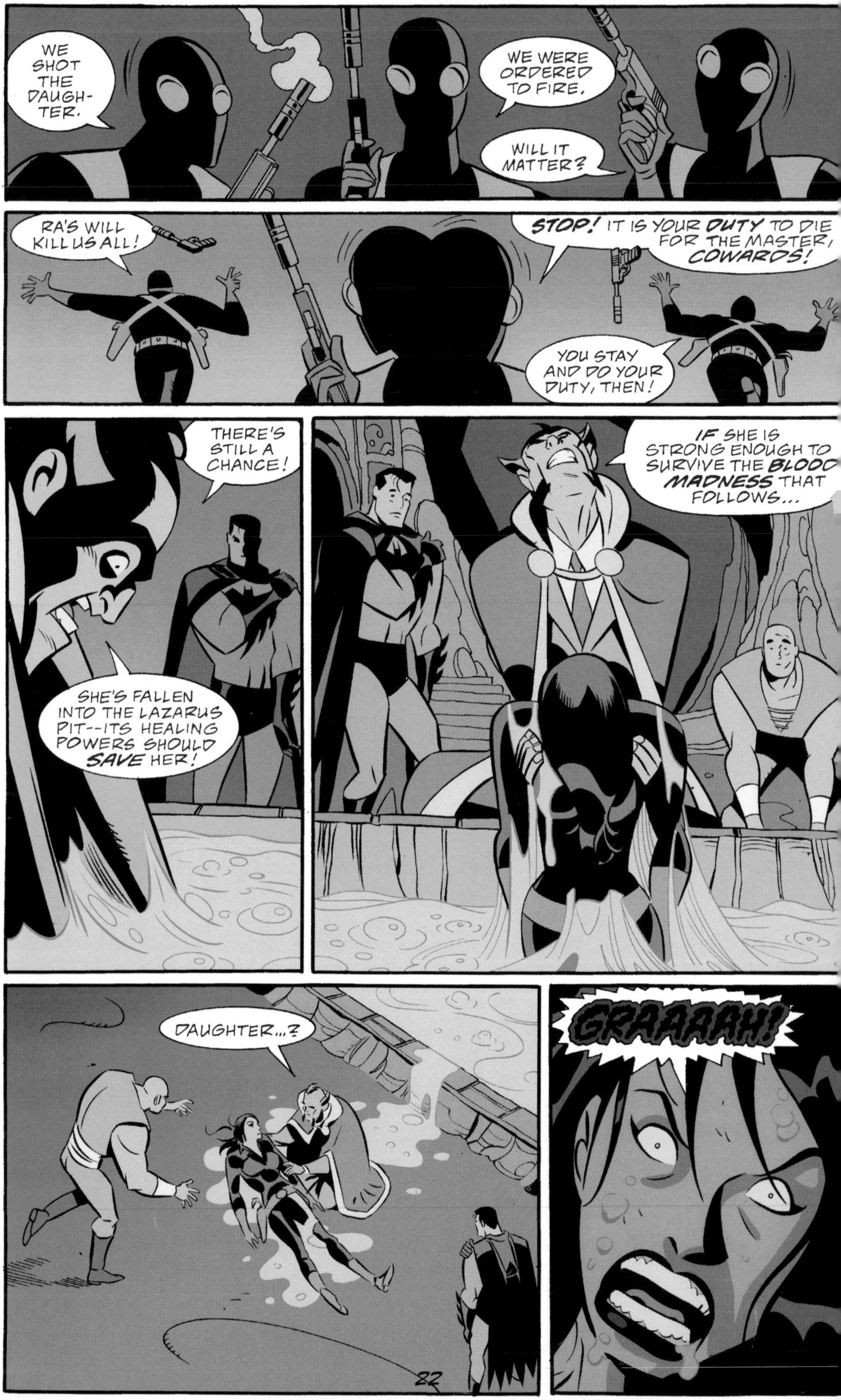

WE SHOT THE DAUGHTER.
WE WERE ORDERED TO FIRE.
WILL IT MATTER?
RA'S WILL KILL US ALL!
STOP! IT IS YOUR DUTY TO DIE FOR THE MASTER, COWARDS!
YOU STAY AND DO YOUR DUTY, THEN!
THERE'S STILL A CHANCE!
SHE'S FALLEN INTO THE LAZARUS PIT--ITS HEALING POWERS SHOULD SAVE HER!
IF SHE IS STRONG ENOUGH TO SURVIVE THE BLOOD MADNESS THAT FOLLOWS...
DAUGHTER...?
GRAAAAH!

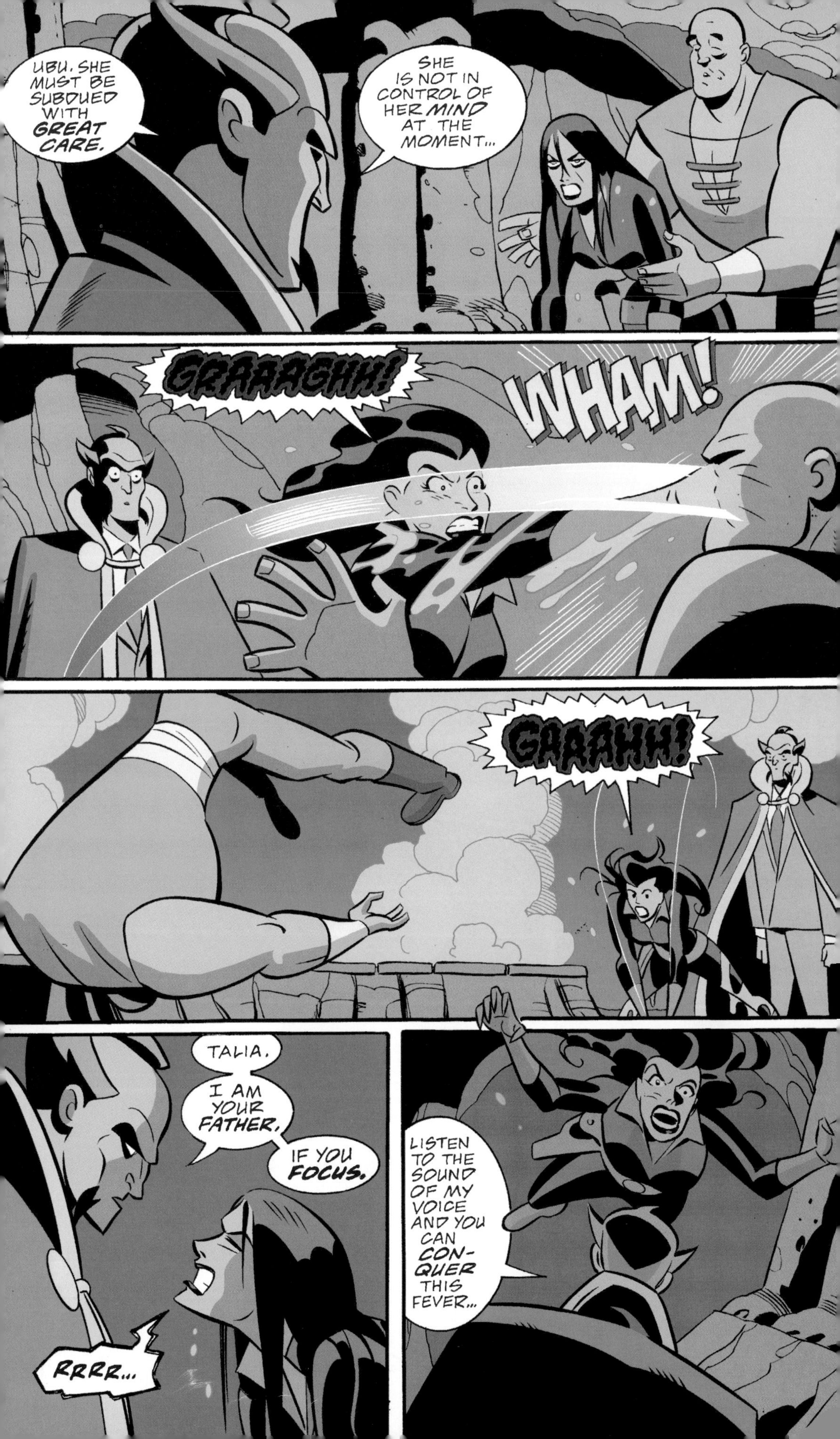
UBU. SHE MUST BE SUBDUED WITH GREAT CARE.
SHE IS NOT IN CONTROL OF HER MIND AT THE MOMENT...
GRAAAGHH!
WHAM!
GAAAHH!
TALIA.
I AM YOUR FATHER.
IF YOU FOCUS.
RRRR...
LISTEN TO THE SOUND OF MY VOICE AND YOU CAN CON-QUER THIS FEVER...

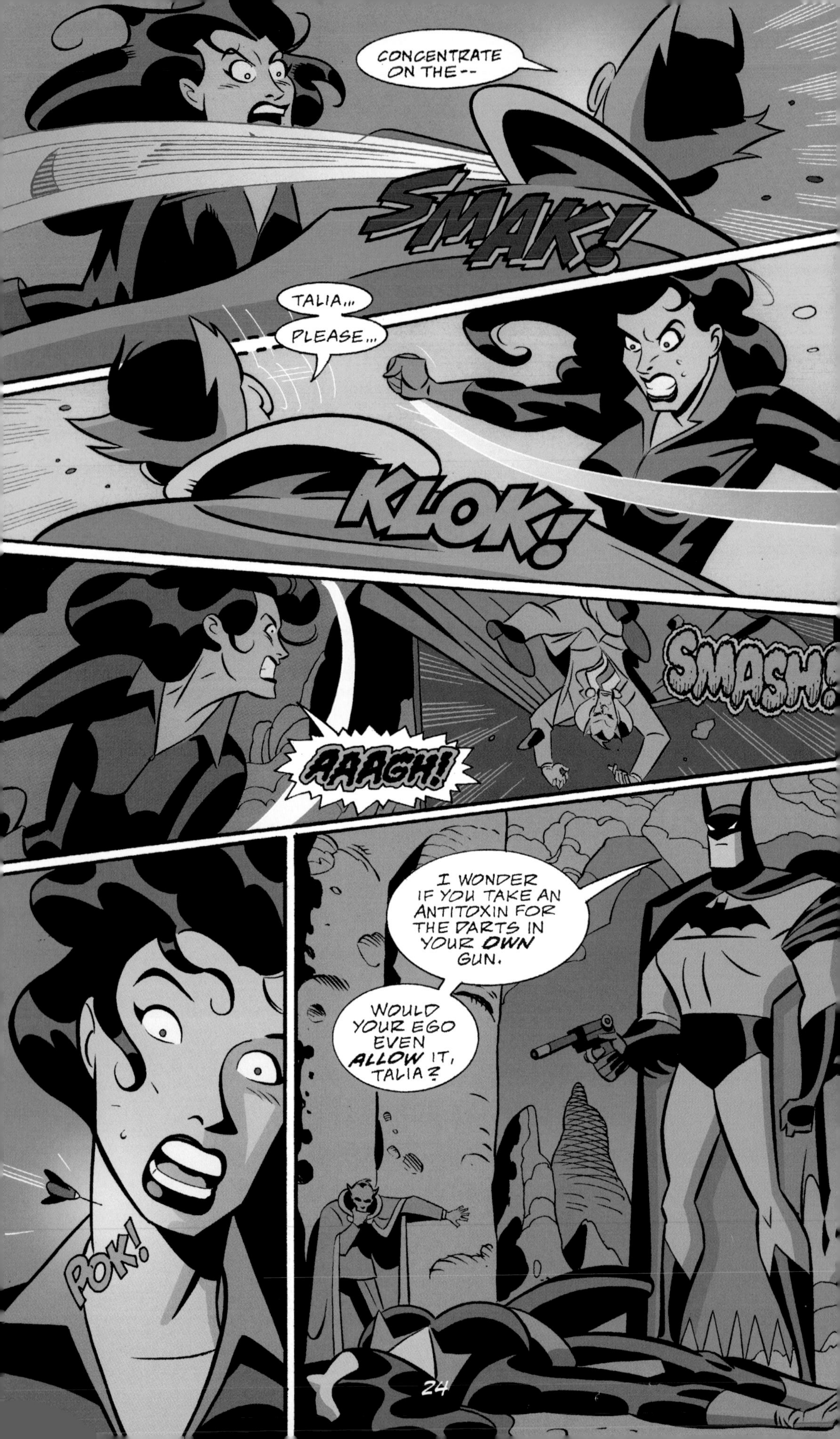

CONCENTRATE ON THE--
SMAK!
TALIA...
PLEASE...
KLOK!
SMASH!
AAAGH!
POK!
I WONDER IF YOU TAKE AN ANTITOXIN FOR THE DARTS IN YOUR OWN GUN.
WOULD YOUR EGO EVEN ALLOW IT, TALIA?

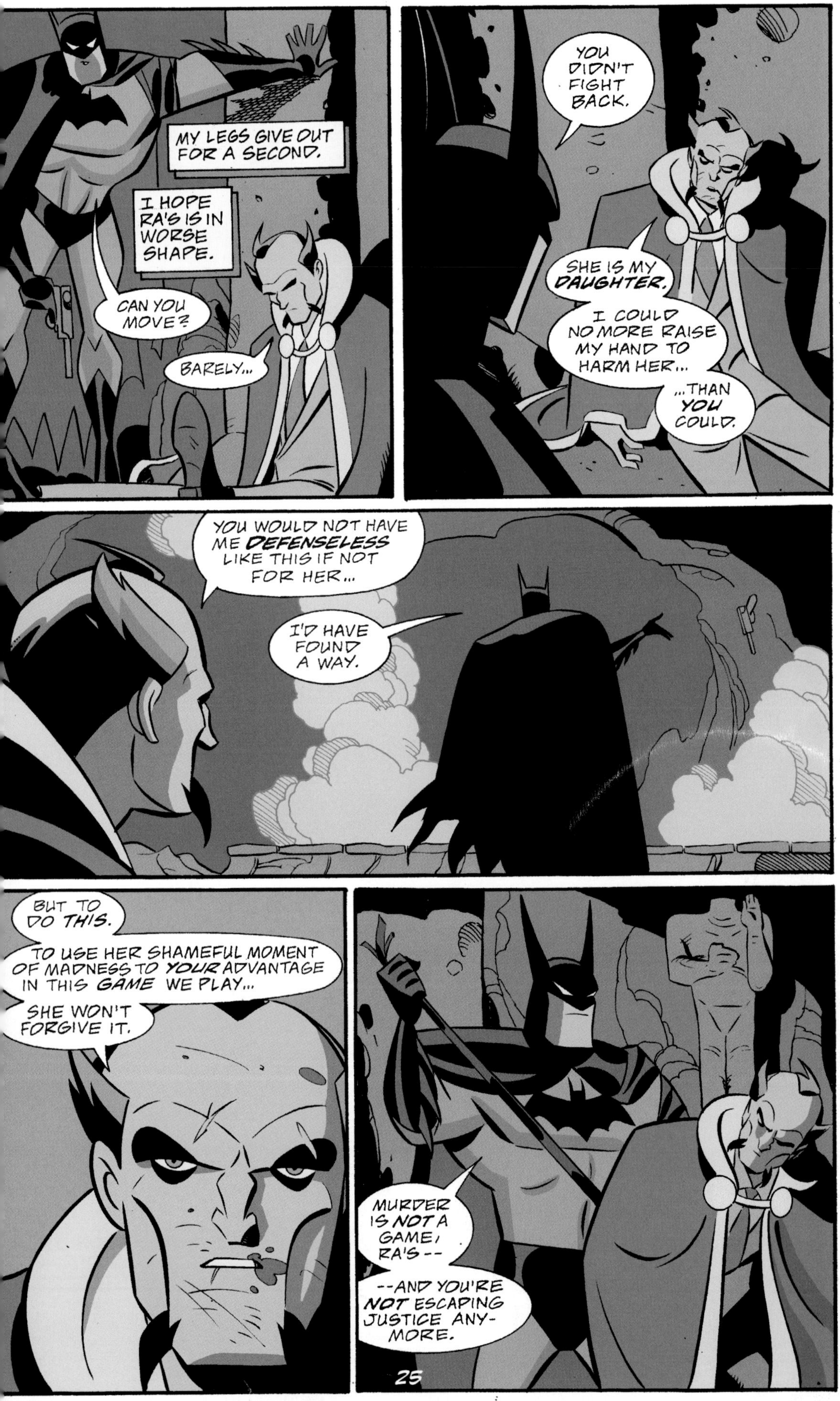
MY LEGS GIVE OUT FOR A SECOND.
I HOPE RA'S IS IN WORSE SHAPE.
CAN YOU MOVE?
BARELY...
YOU DIDN'T FIGHT BACK.
SHE IS MY DAUGHTER.
I COULD NO MORE RAISE MY HAND TO HARM HER...
...THAN YOU COULD.
YOU WOULD NOT HAVE ME DEFENSELESS LIKE THIS IF NOT FOR HER...
I'D HAVE FOUND A WAY.
BUT TO DO THIS.
TO USE HER SHAMEFUL MOMENT OF MADNESS TO YOUR ADVANTAGE IN THIS GAME WE PLAY...
SHE WON'T FORGIVE IT.
MURDER IS NOT A GAME, RA'S --
--AND YOU'RE NOT ESCAPING JUSTICE ANY-MORE.

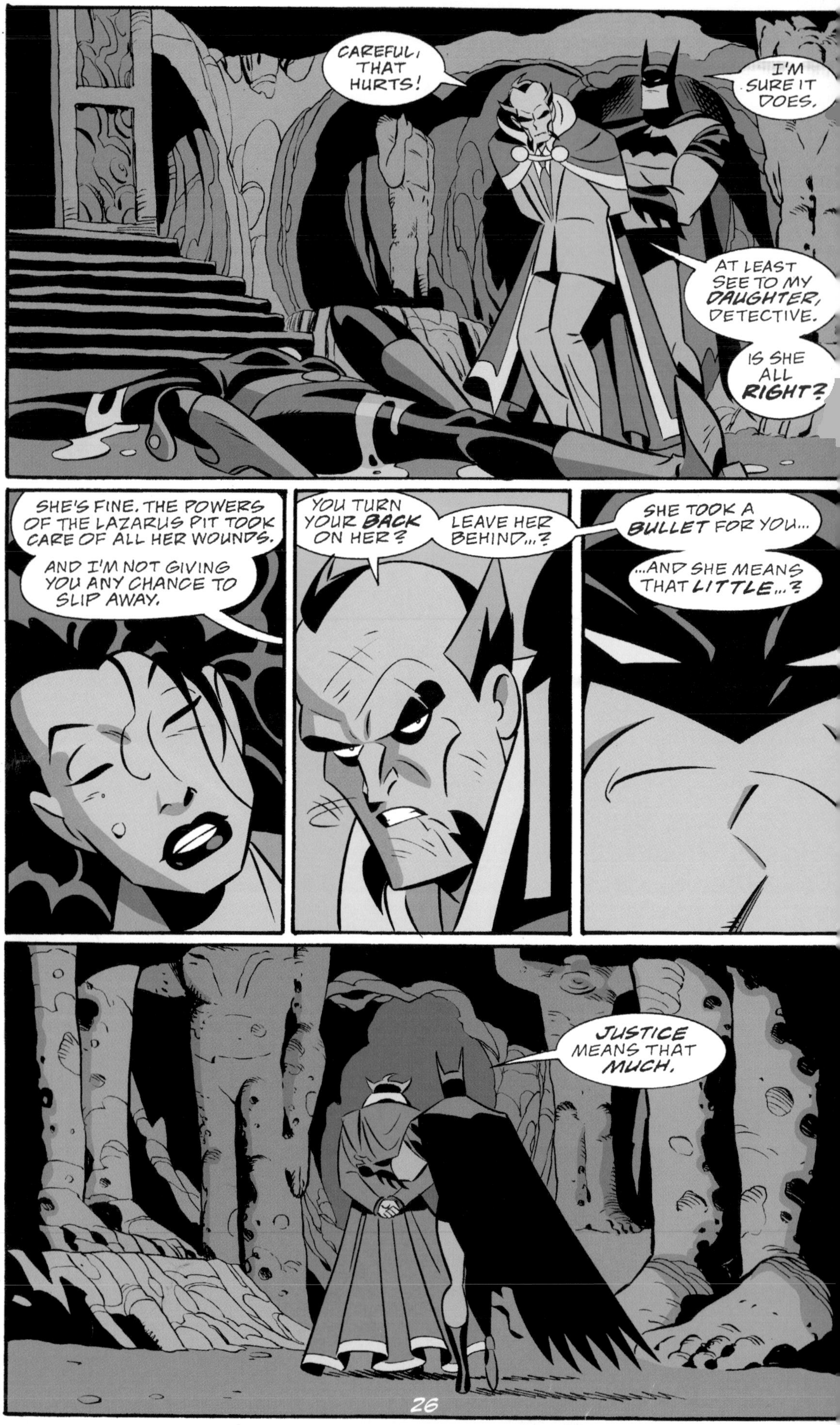
CAREFUL, THAT HURTS!
I'M SURE IT DOES.
AT LEAST SEE TO MY DAUGHTER, DETECTIVE.
IS SHE ALL RIGHT?
SHE'S FINE. THE POWERS OF THE LAZARUS PIT TOOK CARE OF ALL HER WOUNDS.
AND I'M NOT GIVING YOU ANY CHANCE TO SLIP AWAY.
YOU TURN YOUR BACK ON HER?
LEAVE HER BEHIND...?
SHE TOOK A BULLET FOR YOU...
...AND SHE MEANS THAT LITTLE...?
JUSTICE MEANS THAT MUCH.

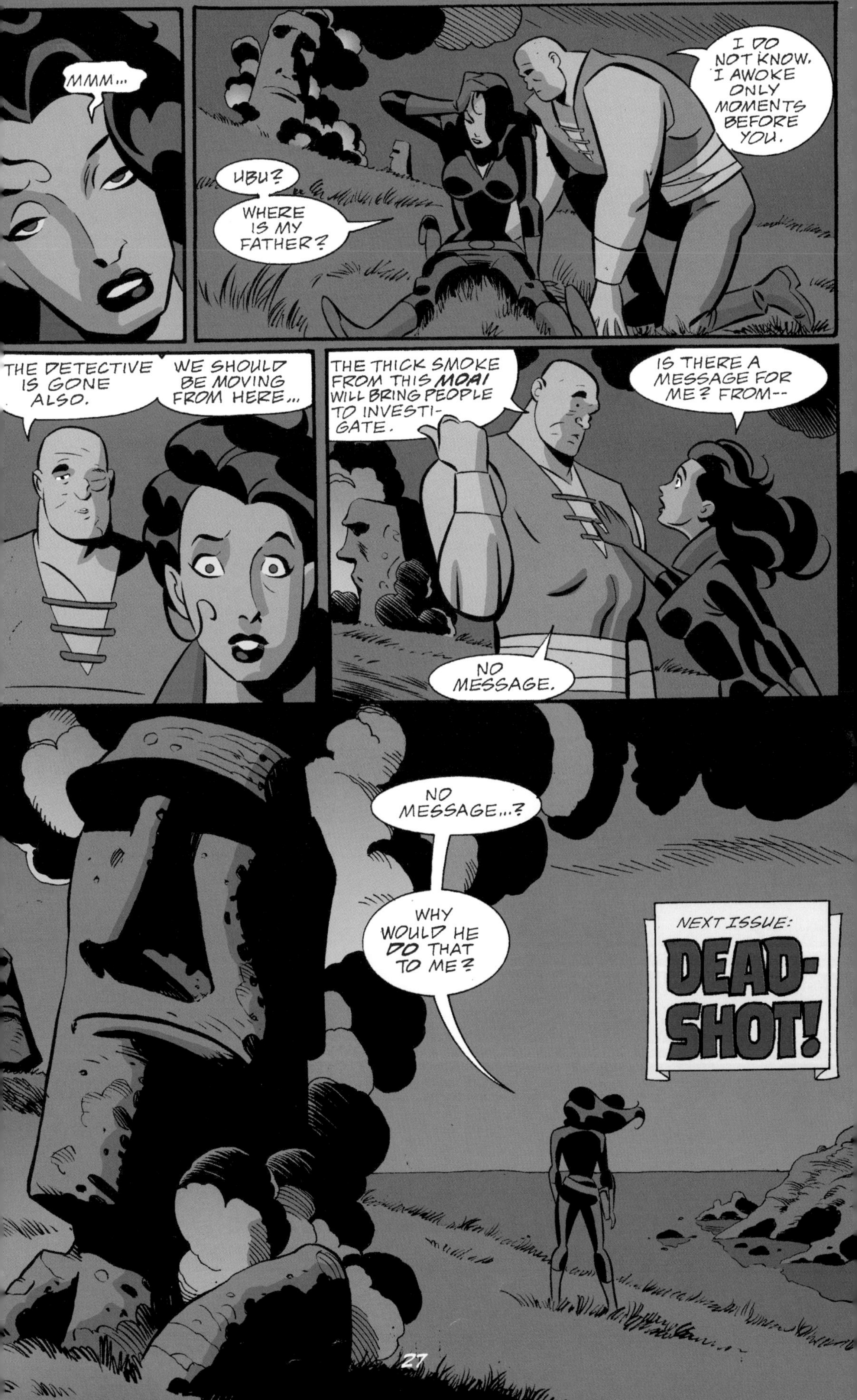
MMM...
UBU?
WHERE IS MY FATHER?
I DO NOT KNOW. I AWOKE ONLY MOMENTS BEFORE YOU.
THE DETECTIVE IS GONE ALSO.
WE SHOULD BE MOVING FROM HERE...
THE THICK SMOKE FROM THIS MOAI WILL BRING PEOPLE TO INVESTI-GATE.
IS THERE A MESSAGE FOR ME? FROM--
NO MESSAGE.
NO MESSAGE...?
WHY WOULD HE DO THAT TO ME?
NEXT ISSUE:
DEAD-SHOT!

CREATORS

TY TEMPLETON WRITER & PENCILLER

Ty Templeton was born in the wilds of downtown Toronto, Canada to a show-business family. He makes his living writing and drawing comic books, working on such characters as Batman, Superman, Spider-Man, The Simpsons, the Avengers, and many others.

DAN SLOTT WRITER

Dan Slott is a comics writer best known for his work on DC Comics' *Arkham Asylum*, and, for Marvel, *The Avengers* and the *Amazing Spider-Man*.

RICK BURCHETT PENCILLER

Rick Burchett has worked as a comics artist for more than 25 years. He has received the comics industry's Eisner Award three times, Spain's Haxtur Award, and he has been nominated for England's Eagle Award. Rick lives with his wife and two sons near St. Louis, Missouri.

TERRY BEATTY INKER

For more than ten years, Terry Beatty was the main inker of DC Comics' "animated-style" Batman comics, including *The Batman Strikes*. More recently, he worked on *Return to Perdition*, a graphic novel for DC's Vertigo Crime.

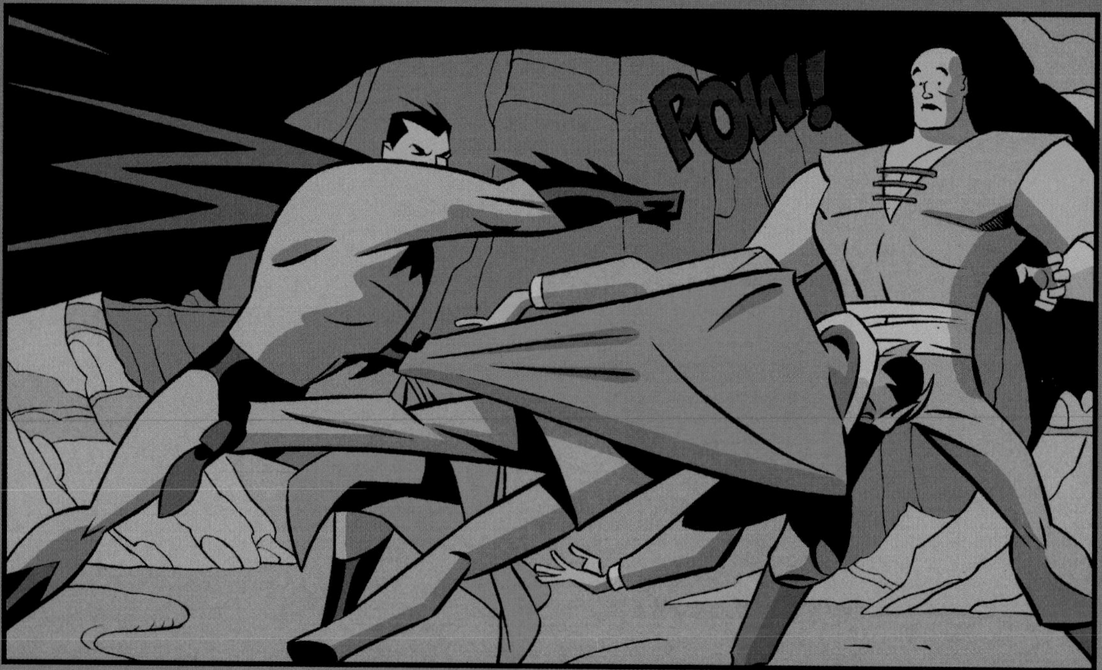
POW!

GLOSSARY

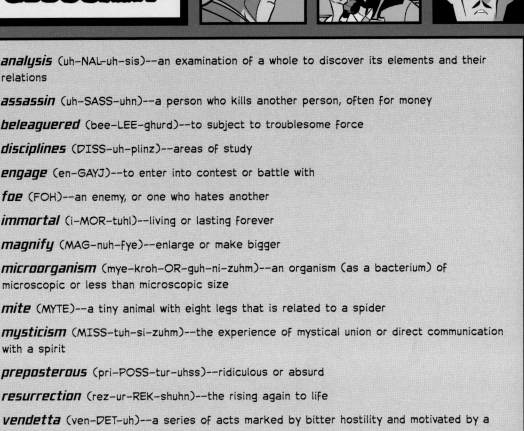

analysis (uh-NAL-uh-sis)--an examination of a whole to discover its elements and their relations

assassin (uh-SASS-uhn)--a person who kills another person, often for money

beleaguered (bee-LEE-ghurd)--to subject to troublesome force

disciplines (DISS-uh-plinz)--areas of study

engage (en-GAYJ)--to enter into contest or battle with

foe (FOH)--an enemy, or one who hates another

immortal (i-MOR-tuhl)--living or lasting forever

magnify (MAG-nuh-fye)--enlarge or make bigger

microorganism (mye-kroh-OR-guh-ni-zuhm)--an organism (as a bacterium) of microscopic or less than microscopic size

mite (MYTE)--a tiny animal with eight legs that is related to a spider

mysticism (MISS-tuh-si-zuhm)--the experience of mystical union or direct communication with a spirit

preposterous (pri-POSS-tur-uhss)--ridiculous or absurd

resurrection (rez-ur-REK-shuhn)--the rising again to life

vendetta (ven-DET-uh)--a series of acts marked by bitter hostility and motivated by a desire for revenge

BATMAN GLOSSARY

Alfred Pennyworth: Bruce Wayne's loyal butler. He knows Bruce Wayne's secret identity and helps the Dark Knight solve crimes in Gotham City.

Batgirl: one of the Dark Knight's crime-fighting partners, secretly Commissioner Gordon's daughter Barbara.

Ra's al Ghul: a centuries-old villain who hopes to save the world by killing most of humanity and ruling the few people who remain.

Robin: one of the Dark Knight's crime-fighting partners, secretly Bruce Wayne's ward Dick Grayson.

Society of Shadows: an organization of highly trained assassins led by Ra's al Ghul.

Talia al Ghul: the daughter of Ra's al Ghul and a member of the Society of Shadows.

VISUAL QUESTIONS & PROMPTS

1. The Dark Knight is an expert martial artist. Find at least two panels in this book where Batman uses this skill. Do you believe he could've solved those problems differently? Explain you answer.

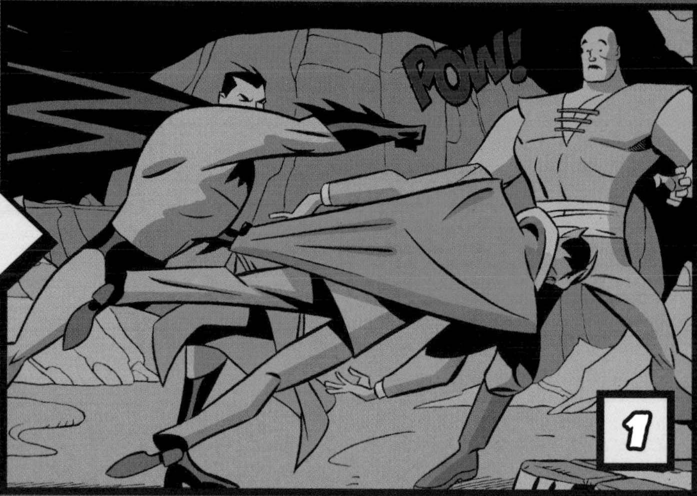
POW!
1

2. Batman has many crime-fighting skills, including the ability to see in the dark. What are some other skills that the Dark Knight has? Find panels in this book where he uses those or other abilities.

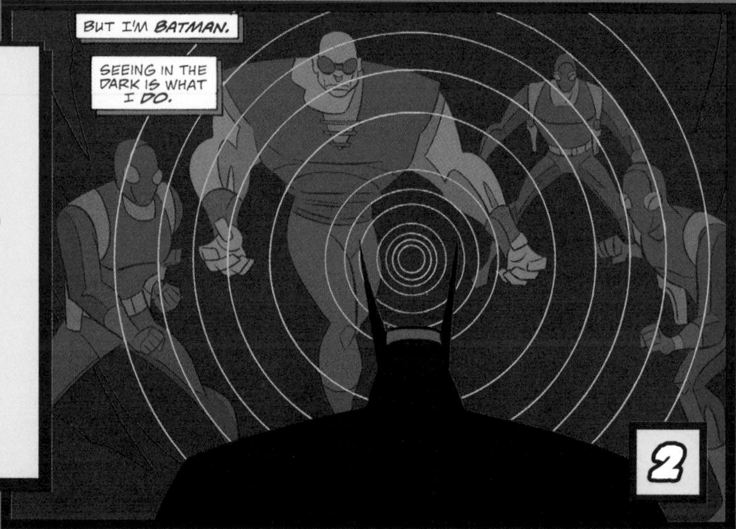
BUT I'M BATMAN.
SEEING IN THE DARK IS WHAT I DO.
2

3. In comic books, sound effects [also known as SFX] are used to show sounds, such as the firing of a gun or other weapon. Make a list of all the sound effects in this book, and then write a definition for each term. Soon, you'll have your own SFX dictionary!

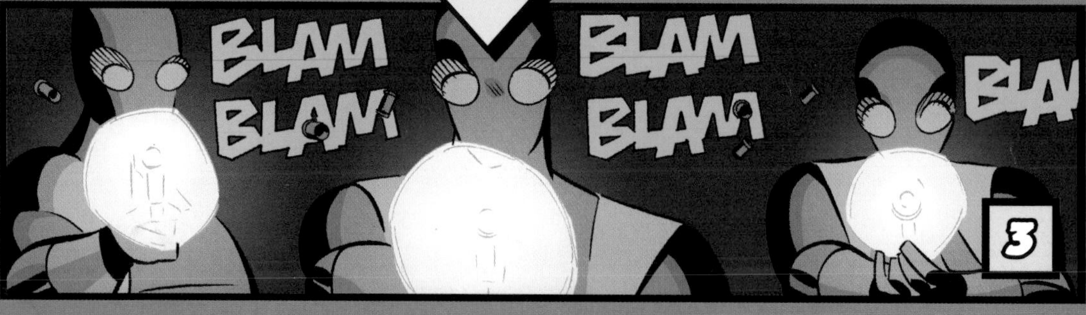
BLAM
BLAM
BLAM
BLAM
3

4. Comic book illustrators draw motion lines (also known as action lines) to show movement of a character or an object, like Talia's fist in the panel below. Find other panels in this book with motion lines. Do you think they make the illustrations more exciting? Why or why not?

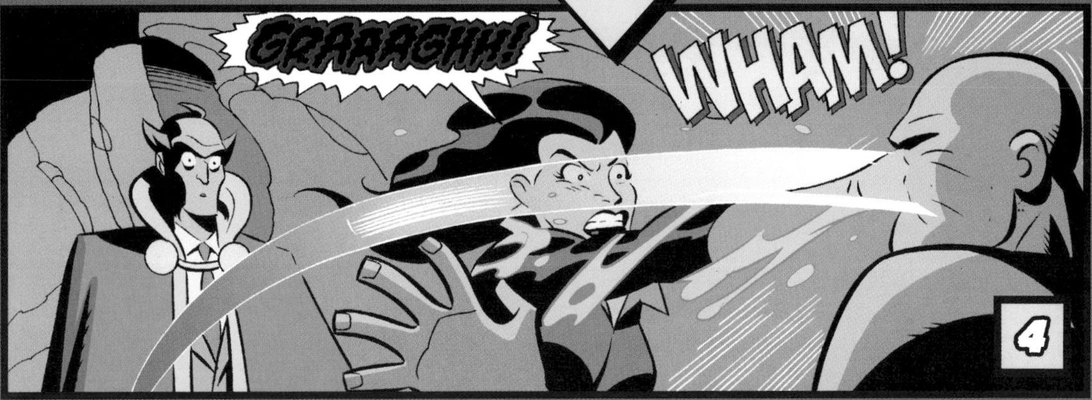
GRAAAGHH!
WHAM!
4

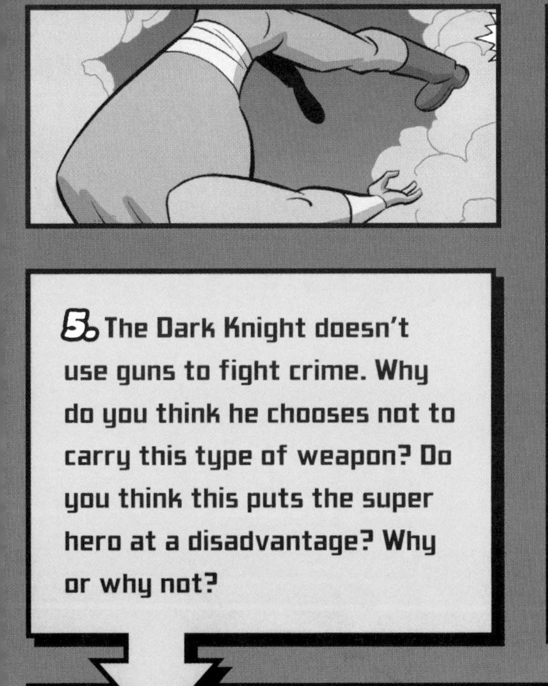

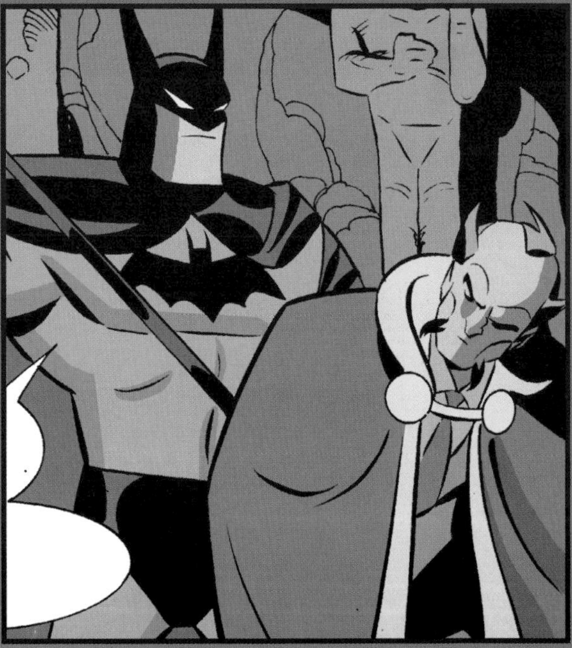

5. The Dark Knight doesn't use guns to fight crime. Why do you think he chooses not to carry this type of weapon? Do you think this puts the super hero at a disadvantage? Why or why not?

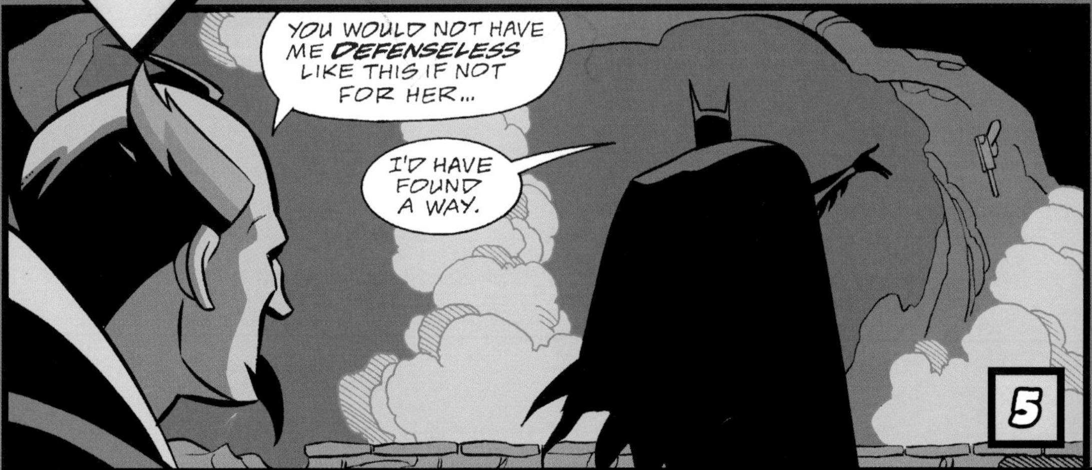
YOU WOULD NOT HAVE ME DEFENSELESS LIKE THIS IF NOT FOR HER...
I'D HAVE FOUND A WAY.
5

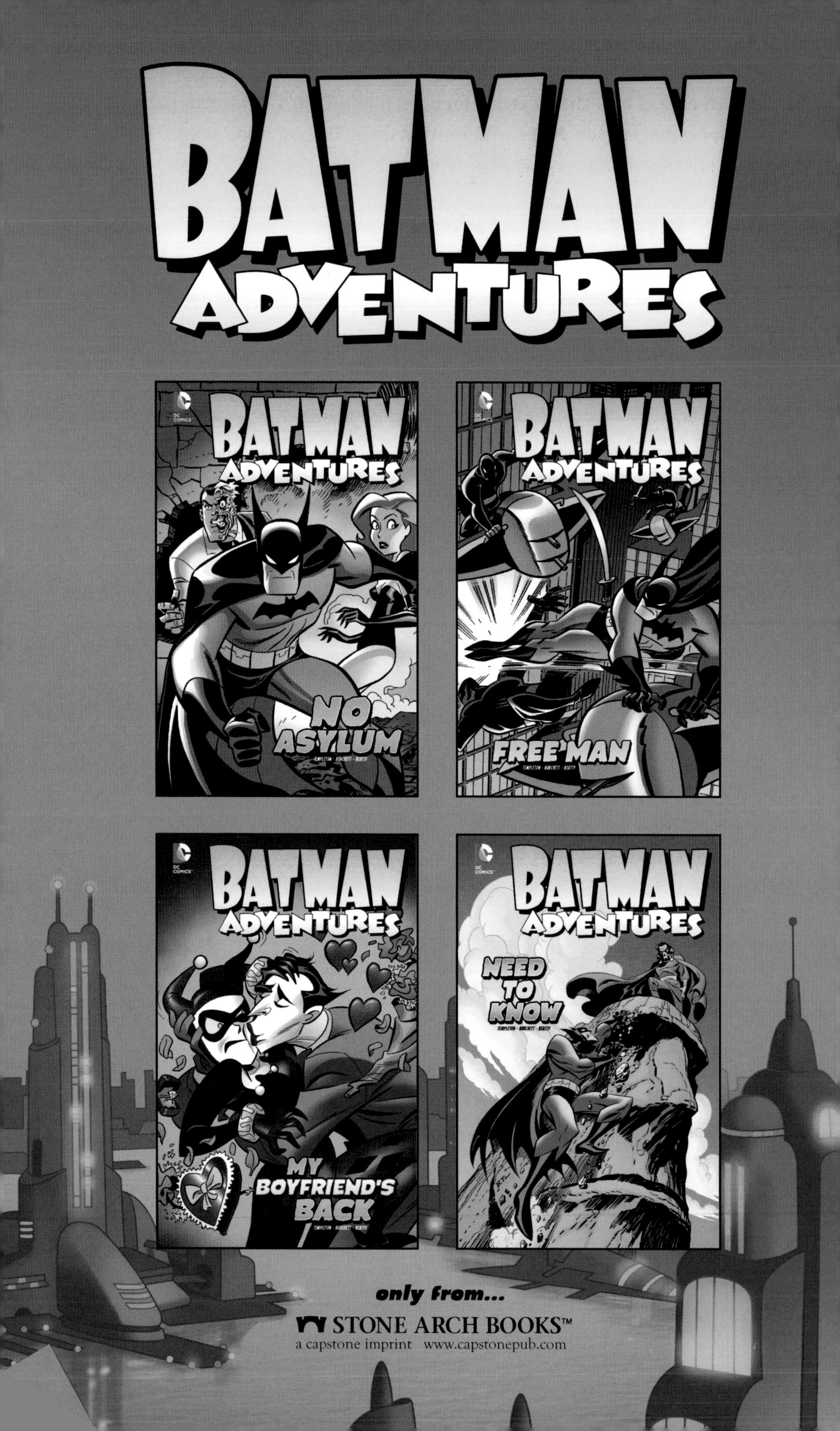
BATMAN ADVENTURES
BATMAN ADVENTURES
NO ASYLUM
BATMAN ADVENTURES
FREE MAN
BATMAN ADVENTURES
MY BOYFRIEND'S BACK
BATMAN ADVENTURES
NEED TO KNOW
only from...
STONE ARCH BOOKS™
a capstone imprint www.capstonepub.com